TRANQUIL HEIGHTS

MEGAN SPEECE

This book features subjects that are intended for mature audiences and may be distressing to some readers including loss of a child, mentions of sexual assault, and suicide.

DEDICATION

For Kori, who was endlessly patient and always willing to talk story with me.

"My sister didn't believe in the paranormal or the supernatural. What she didn't realize is that it wasn't her belief that mattered."

-Katie Edgecomb

ONE

KATIE EDGECOMB'S FRIDAY started much like any other weekday. She ate a quick breakfast of eggs and sweet potato, grabbed her coffee to go, and walked to the preschool at the edge of her neighborhood. It was April 30th, and the weather was unseasonably warm for a Seattle spring. Katie didn't complain about the near constant cloud cover and consistent drizzle of Seattle winters, but she was still overjoyed about the premature return of the sun and the opportunity to leave her coat at home.

She moved around Busy Bees Preschool, preparing the building for the day's activities involving many dozens of sticky fingers, more toddler wipes than seemed appropriate, and the beautiful sound of uncontrolled laughter that children have before they learn to keep themselves small. Katie loved this space. She loved the brightly colored ABCs painted on the wall and the wall of chalkboard paint where little hands drew nonsensical worlds from the imaginations that owned them. She loved the rug that had a built-in street on which miniature cars raced and went to work. But most of all, she loved the children who occupied this space five days a week.

Katie spent the day helping four year olds write their names, refereeing disagreements, and unleashing chaotic creativity upon Busy Bee's art room. Fridays were painting days at Busy Bee and one of Katie's favorites because of its penchant for pandemonium. Many teachers would have ended Paint Fridays when faced with the prospect of so many little hands covered in paint, just dying to share their creation. Katie luxuriated in it. She loved the layers of color that ended up on her own hands as little ones grabbed her and guided her across the room to another finished masterpiece.

Each student's apron started the year as a perfectly plain beige frock. By the end of the year, it was a chaotic myriad of colors, a story of the year's Fridays spelled out in paint. Katie started each year with her own fresh apron, keeping the soiled ones from years past as a sort of yearbook signed by each little soul she had the joy of teaching.

Of course, the problem with Paint Fridays was that the paint didn't always stay on the aprons. The school warned parents at the beginning of every year, and eventually they learned to send their children to school in older clothes, or the clothes that already carried the stains of Paint Friday.

Katie usually wore older paint-worthy clothes on Fridays as well, but this Friday, it was Katie's birthday. After work, she was expected at a party where a Paint Friday outfit would be deemed unacceptable. Katie could tell that the sunny weather was having a positive impact on her students' feelings by the amount of yellow, green, and pink paint that drying on her blouse and jeans. Students had covered large pieces of paper with scenes of flowers growing, boats on the water, and suns shining over tall buildings.

During the afternoon break, she sent a quick text to her husband Jason. *Gonna need you to bring me a new outfit. Paint Friday strikes again.* Her phone buzzed almost immediately, and Jason's reply brought a smile to her face. *Already had an extra outfit hanging in the car's backseat. See you soon.*

Jason was the most thoughtful person Katie had ever met. They'd been in the same environmental science class their sophomore year of college, and he'd chased her down the corridor when she'd left her pencil behind on accident. Katie thought he'd gone through an awful lot of trouble just to return a pencil she could replace at the Dollar Tree, so she asked him if he'd like to get coffee with her. The pencil had been an excuse for Jason to approach Katie, so he'd accepted readily. That pencil encounter quickly grew into a whirlwind romance. Katie felt safe, cared for, and heard when she was with him.

He'd proposed by placing a ring on a pencil and presenting it to her as though she'd dropped it. It was corny and ridiculous but also perfect. They married shortly after graduation and started their adult lives together. Jason was in marketing in a tech firm downtown, and Katie made use of her early childhood education degree in Busy Bees Preschool. Katie wasn't sure how she'd started living the dream, but she was eternally grateful that she was.

The end of the day came quickly—snacks, nap time, free play, and then the alphabetical lineup for a structured pickup. Jason pulled up to Busy Bees just as Katie was handing over the last paint stained, chatty four year old (Yunker, Ainsley) to a bemused parent. Katie waved as the vehicle pulled away and let out a contented sigh as Jason planted a kiss on her cheek and placed his hand over her stomach.

"I can't wait till our own Busy Bee walks home with you, covered in paint every Friday." Jason's happiness was palpable and contagious. Not that Katie needed much of a boost in the happiness department for their future child.

"I can't wait to see Liz's face tonight when I give her this birthday present." Katie half laughed, the excitement shining out of her face. Jason handed her the extra outfit and gestured toward the door of Busy Bee. They had little time to make it to the venue, and Seattle's traffic was a cruel mistress when on a time crunch.

Katie daydreamed about Liz's reaction to her news. Liz and Katie were fraternal twins and enjoyed a seemingly supernatural connection they had deemed "twin sense." Though they had a deep understanding of each other, they couldn't have been more opposite in personality and appearance.

As children, Elizabeth and Katelyn Hanover had gotten into as much precocious trouble as any children could. Liz had always been the mastermind behind whatever ludicrous plot the twins were scheming and dreaming up, but Katie never let Liz take the fall for anything they did. Katie may not have been as mischievous as Liz, but she followed her sister willingly, and often happily, into dangerous territory. She came to Liz's rescue every time they'd been caught in the act (or after the act). If Liz's antics lead to injury, Katie would care for her before their mother ever needed to place a kiss on a scrape.

As adults, Liz's fearlessness morphed into ambition, and Katie's loyalty morphed into nurturing. Liz was a couple months away from finishing her law degree and already had corporate firms in the city courting her. Katie had discovered a love for teaching small children as a teenager, babysitting the neighbor's kids. She'd stuck with that love and found the perfect career for her.

The only thing missing from Katie's life was a baby. This was also Liz's opinion. Liz had never wanted children; she just wasn't much of a nurturing type. She did, however, aim to be the coolest aunt on the face of the planet and had consistently cheered Katie on as she and Jason tried for a baby.

Katie knew it would overjoy Liz that a little Edgecomb would soon debut in the world. Truly, she couldn't think of a much better birthday present for her and Liz than the news of an addition to the family.

TWO

KATIE'S VISION SWAM in bright circles of color as camera flashes flooded the back room of Harley's Pizzeria. She could feel the warm comfort of Liz's body as they squished together to lean over the cake. Her vision cleared after the rousing and spectacularly off-key rendition of "Happy Birthday" came to a close. She spared a glance at Liz's smiling face and drew joy from her sister's sparkling eyes. Liz always looked as though she were sitting on the punchline of a joke or a major piece of good news. Her face shone with joy and a hint of mischief as she bent, pulling Katie down with her to blow out the twenty-five candles on the cake. Applause exploded around them as tiny tendrils of smoke curled into the air above the cake.

As their father, Tim, started cutting and disseminating pieces of the cake, Katie pulled Liz off to the side of the room. Katie was ready to share her secret with her sister; keeping anything from Liz was difficult for Katie. After all, they'd shared everything since the day they'd come screaming into the world.

It was Katie's turn to let her eyes sparkle with mischief as Liz slowly unwrapped the gift, as though she were suspicious that the contents might jump out and bite her. She looked down upon the t-shirt that was carefully folded to show the words "Auntiesaurus Rex." Her faced played quickly through looks of puzzlement, dawning comprehension, and then rapturous joy. Liz launched herself at Katie, practically taking both of them to the ground with her exuberance.

"Jason and I aren't telling anyone else yet, so keep it a secret. It's still early, but I just couldn't keep this from you." Katie laughed as she hugged Liz.

"Cross my heart and hope to die," Liz replied, making the X motion over her heart as she pulled away. "I'm so thrilled for you. Your life is finally your literal dream. How lucky are you?"

"How lucky are *we*?" Katie said, looping an arm

through her sister's and turning them to look out at the room of their family and friends.

The crowd was a delightful mix of corporate suits, denim vests decked out in spikes and patches, and brightly colored, comfortable chic. The corporate suits were mostly Katie and Liz's mutual friends. Their father was a partner in a large corporate law firm, and the twins had made friends with the other lawyers' children at company retreats and picnics through the years. The spikes and patches were all Liz. Despite her ambitions to be a corporate lawyer like their father, she had never let go of her alternative style.

Even now, just months from graduation and with multiple firms ready to make her offers, her pixie haircut held streaks of bright pink. She wore a perfectly tailored black pantsuit over a bandeau top. Liz had dubbed herself a "corporate punk" and threw herself wholeheartedly into her eclectic fashion and personality mix. The suit drew attention to Liz's angular features. There had always been something hard about Liz, both physically and emotionally. She was all sharp angles and sinewy muscle on the outside. Liz kept a rigorous exercise schedule. Just looking at the gym selfies on Liz's Instagram made Katie tired.

Internally, Liz was highly skeptical of the entire

world. She was slow to trust, with a keen sense and little patience for bullshit. Katie knew she was going to be a shark in the courtroom, and she was frequently grateful that Liz was always in her corner instead of the opposite.

Katie was a good balance for Liz, in all things. Where Liz was hard and angular, Katie was soft and round. It wasn't that Katie was large; both twins were five foot four and small of frame. Katie didn't much care for the gym and opted for slow and steady walks on trails and beaches. There was a softness to her body that showed that she was much more likely to be lifting books than weights, and she was perfectly okay with that. Her blonde hair fell in soft and often unruly waves to her shoulders, though it lived most of its life caged in a high ponytail. She was more open to the world and could more readily accept things that didn't have an explanation. Katie attributed her openness to consistently looking at the world through the lens of her students, who still found wonder and fascination in the smallest things.

Katie fit right in with the brightly colored, comfortable chic faction of the guests. They were her friends from college, teachers from other preschools in the area, and women from the hiking book club she ran. Each month, she led a group of ten women on an easy hike that ended in a picnic and the discussion of the month's book. Her blouse was a flowy boho affair in a sunny yellow that made her hair look lighter than it really was. Paired with stretch skinny jeans and flats in the same shade, she looked like she'd be more at home at a festival or beach than a party in the city.

"This party looks like Ms. Frizzle took the principal to a Green Day concert," Liz said, eyes dancing wickedly. Katie looked into her sister's face, trying to determine exactly how much trouble they were about to cause.

Despite the differences in their appearance, there was one attribute that made it obvious they were sisters. They both had eyes in a strange shade of blue that was almost gray, and sometimes held hints of darkest green. Jason had told her that her eyes were like the ocean just after a storm when the sun was peeking out from behind the dark clouds. Looking at her sister, Katie recognized what an apt description that was. Except, at this moment, Katie was pretty sure the storm was just brewing and had not yet passed.

"Liz, what have you cooked up now?" Katie asked, eyes roving the pizzeria for booby traps. Liz widened her eyes and smiled sweetly, the perfect picture of innocence.

She was still smiling sweetly at Katie as their mother, Angela, and their maternal grandmother, Virginia, walked up. Angela was beaming, ever the delightful hostess. Only a slight tightness around her eyes showed she was wrestling with other emotions. Virginia was more open with her emotions. Her lined face set in a grim pattern made her look even older than she was.

"I can't believe my babies are twenty five," Angela said, voice thick as she tried to hold back tears. She laid a hand on each of the twins' faces, her eyes dancing over them, memorizing every line and curve.

Angela's face lost its pretense of happiness, and her striking resemblance to her mother moved Katie unexpectedly. She wondered if she was looking into the future as Angela spoke again.

"Promise me you'll hold on to this memory. And to the memories of your childhood. Life is so cruel and unfair, and you may not always have each other. "

Liz groaned aloud and Katie felt her sister's body stiffen, the tension singing down the arm that touched her own.

"Mom, please," Katie said quietly. "Today isn't the day for your superstitions and sad stories."

"Today is exactly the day," Grandma Virginia

said, voice hard and ever so slightly tinged with fear. She pulled a silver cross out from under her floral sweater and tugged it back and forth on its chain, as though the movement were a type of silent prayer.

Angela waved her mother off and nodded a little too fast. "Of course, girls. You are happy today, and that's all a mother really wants for her daughters. But please at least promise me you'll be careful on your way home tonight." Angela wiped her palms on her thighs, smoothing non-existent wrinkles out of her tasteful black cocktail dress.

After many platitudes and promises to be careful—"We won't drive after we've been drinking. You know us better than that. No, Mom, we won't light any candles at home tonight. We'll take the stairs, not he elevator."— Angela gave her daughters a wistful smile and drifted off into the party, Virginia in tow. Katie felt Liz let out a gust of air and turned to look at her sister, her head shaking and a laugh building deep in her chest.

"I am so glad that after tonight we will never have to hear their superstitious drivel again!" Liz exclaimed.

Their mother and grandmother had been pounding family superstitions into their heads since they were young. They had been scared at first, spending many a night shoved into Liz's twin size bed, holding onto each other for fear that one of them may disappear. As they entered their teenage years, they realized that the family's superstitions did not differ from any other tales meant to scare children into behaving. They no more believed in the family "curse" than they believed in witches that lived in candy houses and ate children.

Before Katie could respond, Liz had jumped up on the nearest table despite wearing black studded Jeffrey Campbell ankle boots gave her an extra five inches of height. Katie groaned and covered her face, peeking at Liz through her fingers like a child watching a horror movie. The noise in the small space ceased as the guests noticed Liz's appearance high above the crowd.

"Friends and family, Katie and I are so glad you all are here. It truly wouldn't be a birthday celebration without you all." Liz paused for a smattering of applause and whistles. "However, this party is looking just a tad bit predictable, and you all know how much I hate predictability." The crowd let out a collective groan sprinkled with laughter, and Katie could see a ripple of movement throughout the room as the guests shuffled their feet anxiously.

"Don't worry, though!" Liz continued as though the ripple of movement was associated with a concern that Liz was correct about their predictability rather than a concern about what she was going to do next. "I've come up with a perfect way to slay this predictability! We're going to have a top swap!"

"What's a top swap?" Katie asked, face still hidden behind her hands. A faint chuckle came from the guests standing closest to her.

"I am so glad you asked, Katie! Everyone is going to pick someone else and ask to trade tops with them. This can be a shirt or outerwear; I won't be that picky. If you refuse to trade garments, you will need to make your way to the bar where the good bartender Vanessa will pour you a shot. Throughout the night, you can ask anyone to trade tops with you. There's no limit. That also means there's no limit to the number of times you could say no and punish yourself with a shot." Liz's eyes gleamed as the guests launched into a din of noise ranging from groans to loud brays of laughter.

Liz jumped down from the table to land in front of Katie, eyes alight with humor and excitement. She removed her tailored suit jacket, stripping down to just her bandeau with brazen nonchalance. This moment would be the perfect way to explain what Liz was like to anyone who asked.

"Alright, give me that yellow sunshiney boho

top. I want to live like Ms. Frizzle," Liz said, holding her jacket out to Katie.

Katie sighed but pulled her top over her head in a graceful slide, exposing the nude cami she was wearing underneath. "You know, it's really unfair of you to do this when you know I can't say no because I can't do the shots," she whispered as she buttoned her sister's jacket.

"Katie, I didn't even know you were pregnant when I decided this was going to be this year's birthday shenanigan."

"I don't believe you."

Liz simply laughed in response and threaded her arm through Katie's before dragging her back into the party. They hugged old friends, traded more tops than they could count, and Liz did shots despite never saying no to a top swap. Katie vaguely noticed their mother's eyes following them around the room, a deep crease forming between her eyebrows. She pointed this out to Liz but immediately regretted it when Liz sang Stevie Wonder's *Superstition* on the karaoke machine.

.   .   .

The party had continued full tilt until Harley— owner of Harley's Pizzeria and family friend—had all but kicked them out so he could clean up to prepare for the next day and "just maybe get some sleep." Katie and Jason had poured Liz, who had perhaps over-imbibed, into an Uber and stayed behind to help Harley clean.

Two hours later, Jason was jiggling the key in the lock of their apartment door. Katie was still humming *Superstition* to herself as she and Jason entered the elevator in their apartment building. She was bone tired as she made her way to their bedroom, eager to get out of her clothes (her own jeans, but someone else's top) and crawl into their bed. As she was pulling back the sheets, her cell phone, still tucked away in her purse, started ringing shrilly.

"Who would call at two a.m.?" Jason asked around his toothbrush and mouthful of toothpaste.

Katie shrugged as she fumbled with the latch on her purse. The number was one she didn't recognize, and if it was a telemarketer, she was going to scream at them. She answered on the last ring and listened to the voice on the other end while looking at Jason. She felt her eyes grow wider and her blood run cold before she heard herself say, "Yes, of course. I'll be right there."

THREE

KATIE SAT IN A TINY WAITING ROOM at the hospital. She had a death grip on Jason's hand and stared at the door, waiting for something—anything—to happen. The voice on the phone had told her there had been an accident involving Liz, who had Katie listed as the emergency contact, and the hospital needed her to come down. The voice had also told her it was okay to call any other family, so as Jason had driven them to the hospital, she had called her mother.

Angela, Virginia, and Katie's father Tim sat silently in chairs across from Katie and Jason, their hands clasped in their laps. The room was painfully quiet, and the ticking of the clock seemed to grow louder with each passing second.

Katie was growing increasingly frustrated. She

had been in this room for twenty minutes and no one had told her anything. Why call her at two in the morning, tell her to rush down here, and then just leave her waiting? As she prepared to get out of her chair and go in search of answers, the door finally opened.

A doctor with a kind face and a man in a well-tailored suit stepped into the room. The doctor introduced himself as Dr. Woodward and the man in the suit was Mr. Grady, the voice on the phone, from hospital administration. Jason introduced himself and each person in the room. Katie wondered if it was unnerving to have all three of the women staring at you, the same look of trepidation playing upon such similar faces. If it was, Dr. Woodward didn't show it. He'd shaken each hand firmly and met their eyes with neutral confidence.

"Katie, Mr. Grady told you there had been an accident involving your sister on the phone. We aren't permitted to give more information over the phone, which is why we needed you to come down here."

"Where is my daughter? Can we go see her?" Angela asked with a hard voice, ready to advocate for her child. Katie knew the question was futile. She could feel it in the way something heavy seemed to have settled in her stomach and in the silence in her mind that used to hold some spark she associated with

Liz. They were in this room because no one was ever going to see Liz again.

"I'm afraid that you cannot see her, Mrs. Hanover. As the Uber carrying your daughter home drove down Sixth Street, a crane holding a beam for new construction experienced a catastrophic failure. The beam landed on the car. Your daughter didn't survive that accident, but I can tell you she likely didn't feel any pain." Dr. Woodward had a nice, calm voice, and sympathetic eyes. Katie wondered vaguely if that meant they chose him over other doctors to deliver this kind of blow to frightened people waiting in quiet little rooms.

"What time?" Angela asked.

Dr. Woodward raised his eyebrows, startled. "I'm sorry?" he questioned.

"What time did the beam fall on my daughter, Doctor? I know it seems silly, but I wouldn't ask if I didn't think it important." A thread of tension ran between her and Virginia.

The doctor blinked twice but regained his composure and looked down at the papers in his hands. "Witnesses report that the accident occurred at 11:58 pm."

"11:58 pm on the day she turned twenty five," Katie whispered. "Fuck."

Everyone turned to look at Katie. Her mother and

grandmother gave her knowing eyes filled with generations of knowledge and sadness. Katie slumped in her chair, mind racing. The grim set of Virginia's face seemed like it had become permanent, as though no one would ever see another expression on her face again. It startled Katie to find the same grim expression taking hold of her mother's face as well. She wondered if this was a mirror into her future, if some day she would become a grim-looking woman, wavy blonde hair streaked with silver, stormy blue eyes sunken and surrounded by wrinkles that showed decades of worry.

Her grandmother had once been soft like she was. She had seen photos. Now she was all hard edges, but not the way Liz had been. No, her hard edges came from years of worry wasting her away until her softness had succumbed to the anxiety. Her mother was hard the way Liz was. Would the anxiety eat away at her, too, until she became a skeletal shell? Would the wavy blonde hair that all the women in their family had become brittle and coarse like straw?

Katie didn't think she believed in curses. She and Liz had been scoffing at the very idea of the curse upon the women in their family for more than a decade now. But Liz was the fourth firstborn daughter to die on her twenty-fifth birthday in their family. Could this big of a coincidence really be just a coincidence?

.   .   .

The next two weeks went by in a whirlwind of funeral arrangements, casseroles, and sympathy cards. Katie functioned on auto-pilot, doing things because they needed to be done. She would likely have stayed in bed or stared at walls for countless hours without a checklist of things that needed doing.

The service was a fine service, well attended, filled with Liz's favorite flowers. Katie didn't think Liz would have much liked it. She was pretty sure her sister would have hated seeing everyone dressed all in black, being so purposefully somber. Liz had been full of life, effervescent. She would have wanted a party with color and streamers and probably something ostentatious, like fireworks. But funerals weren't really about the dead, they were about the living. And the living overwhelmingly felt that somber was the appropriate choice for saying goodbye.

As Jason and Tim said goodbye to the last of people who had attended the wake, Katie found herself alone in her childhood kitchen with Angela and Virginia. Katie had been wrestling with her beliefs for two weeks, trying to make sense of Liz's tragic death and what it meant that she died at twenty five. She didn't want to believe in the family curse. It had always seemed outright ridiculous to her and Liz. That the firstborn daughters of the three previous generations had died on their twenty-fifth birthdays seemed like a coincidence. A strange one, to be sure, but still a coincidence. But now Katie wasn't so sure. Four women in the same family, all firstborn daughters dying on their twenty-fifth birthday? How could that possibly be merely a coincidence?

Katie took a deep, centering breath. "How did it start? The curse?" She kept her eyes on the counter, not willing to see the knowledge on her mother's face. Angela and Virginia went still, prey animals trying not to be seen by the predator, and the tension in the room rose to an uncomfortable level.

"I don't know all the specifics to the answer. I just know that something happened when my grandmother, your great-great grandmother Darrington, worked at Tranquil Heights. You know, the old mental hospital? It's a school now. She said something happened with a patient, something bad. She wouldn't tell me more than that. She just told me it was true, and to be prepared." Virginia took a shuddering breath before continuing. "My mother was Grandma Darrington's firstborn daughter. She died at twenty-five, when I was only five. For many years, I thought that Grandma Darrington had made up a story to explain to me why my mother had died. She hadn't been sick. She was perfectly healthy, perfectly happy. She lost her footing on a tall balcony and fell over the railing. It was a terrible tragedy. A senseless accident. It's hard for small children to understand these things, so I was sure that Grandma was inventing fantastic stories to help me cope.

"And then my own older sister, Mary, died at twenty five in a house fire. The fire department said faulty wiring in the dining room caused the fire. A true accident that no one saw coming. Grandma Darrington used it as another example of the curse. Even then, I was skeptical of it. It just seemed like a strange coincidence to me. And then..." She cut off with a strangled cry.

"Your Aunt Anita wanted to go rafting for her twenty-fifth birthday. It sounded like a wonderful idea to everyone," Angela picked up the story, squeezing her mother's hand. "I was pregnant with you and Liz, so I waited at the exit point while everyone else went on the adventure. They hit a rapid wrong and the raft went flying, dunking everyone into the river. They all made their way to shore, except for Anita. They found her later that day. Her shirt had gotten caught on a jagged rock under the water and she couldn't make it back up to the surface."

Katie had heard the story before, but she and Liz had looked at it as just an accident. So many accidents, tragedies, for just one family to bear. "Say I believe this is a curse," she said slowly. "If we traced the curse back to its origins, could we break it?"

"We've thought of it before. We tried everything we could to get Grandma Darrington to tell us more of the circumstances of it before she died. She absolutely refused. I've no idea why she wouldn't tell us more. Maybe she thought it was unbreakable. Or that merely talking about it gave it more power," Virginia answered bitterly. She tucked a stray piece of hair that had fallen from her tight bun behind her ear, and Katie noticed her face had moved past grim into a sinking sadness that deepened the lines on her face. She wasn't even seventy yet, but so many losses had weighed heavily on her.

"I mean, what even did you try to do? Did you go to Tranquil Heights?"

"I did, when Anita and Angela were small. I tried talking with grandma's coworkers. Asking about bad things that had happened with patients. But that was a broad question. So many bad things happened there over the years that Grandma worked there. It was impossible for any of the coworkers to narrow it down without more specific questions," Virginia answered.

"And you, Mom?" Katie gesticulated at her mother. "You watched Liz and I stop believing. You let us stop believing!" Katie was shouting, angry, and scared.

"I didn't let you stop believing. I've been telling you the same story for your whole life. Liz had a mind of her own. She was so skeptical. She didn't believe in anything even remotely weird. And you followed her through fire," Angela said quietly, eyes pleading. She reached her hand across the counter to grab hold of Katie, but Katie jerked her hand away, forming a tight fist at her side.

"You could have done something to prove it to us. If we would have known we could have done something, we could have figured it out and broken this curse. But instead, you just watched us believe it was all fake, and now Liz is dead."

"Baby, no. If I would have thought, for even one minute, that you and Liz could have changed this fate, I would have done anything. But we've picked through this thing with a fine-tooth comb. There's nothing to find. We gave up trying to solve this before you even stopped believing in it," Angela said, voice thick with tears.

"So, what, we're just supposed accept that every single mother who has girls in our family is going to lose a child? That's ridiculous." Katie edged closer to panic as she thought about the life growing inside her at that very moment. What if that child was a girl? Could she go through with the pregnancy knowing that she may only get twenty-five years with her child? Could she live through twenty-five years of wondering if the curse was real or not? Could she live if it was, and her child died?

FOUR

KATIE WAS CAREFULLY FOLDING CLOTHES into a duffle bag when Jason returned home from work. He leaned against the doorjamb and watched her putter between the closet and the bag on the bed, keeping her attention on her packing while she spoke.

"I've taken a leave of absence from work."

"Are you taking a leave of absence from me?" Jason asked mildly.

Katie looked up at him quickly, eyes wide under raised eyebrows. "No, of course not. Why would you think that?"

Jason cocked an eyebrow and gestured with his palm upward toward the duffle bag.

"Oh." Katie half chuckled as she looked down at

her half-packed bag. "No. I'm not leaving you. I'm going to Tranquil Heights."

"Okay." Jason drew a deep breath as he stepped into the room and took a seat on the bed. "Correct me if I'm wrong, but you've never really been interested in teaching teenagers."

"I'm not going to Tranquil Heights to teach." Katie placed the sweater she'd been gripping into the duffle bag before giving him full eye contact. "I'm going there to figure out this family curse." It was Jason's turn to give her a surprised expression. She took a deep breath and filled her cheeks before forcefully blowing it out. "Look, Jason, I know I've always said the curse was nonsense. And I know you don't believe in this stuff, the supernatural or paranormal or whatever you want to call it. But Liz's death... it has me questioning everything I thought I knew."

"Of course it has. Your twin sister died, Katie. I'd be more concerned if you weren't questioning your entire life right now. Just explain to me exactly what you expect to find at Tranquil Heights."

"Okay." Katie sighed in relief. "The only thing Mom and Grandma know is that Great-Great-Grandma Darrington worked at Tranquil Heights and, while she was there, something bad happened with a patient. After that, every firstborn daughter in our family has died at twenty five."

"Right, okay. But Katie, you and Liz were twins."

"She was born two minutes before me, Jason." An uncomfortable silence stretched between them, growing heavy. "Two minutes is enough for her to be firstborn. And she died on our twenty-fifth birthday. Two fucking minutes before it would not be our birthday anymore. I mean... either it's a curse or there's a god out there with a wicked sense of irony." Katie's voice was heated and her jaw flexed as she gritted her teeth. The circumstances angered her, and it was all she could do to keep from yelling and taking that anger out on the man in front of her.

"So you go to Tranquil Heights and what? Anyone who knew what happened is probably dead. And if they aren't, what are the odds they still work there? It's not even a hospital anymore."

"They have a museum. I called and spoke to someone there. And apparently, they are very meticulous about keeping the records and making sure the history of Tranquil Heights remains public. I've also arranged to stay for a few days while I do the research." She ran her hands over the sweater at the top of the bag, smoothing nonexistent wrinkles.

"And what will the research do?" Jason placed his hand over hers, stilling them. "So, you get more backstory about your great-great-grandmother. Maybe you find out about this patient. Then what?"

"I break the curse." Katie whispered. Despite the quiet words, there was a fierceness in the set of her jaw and the shine of her eyes that Jason recognized.

"And if there is no curse?" He knew it was futile to argue, but he couldn't bring himself to let this go.

"Then I've done something crazy that hasn't hurt anyone else, I guess." She shook her head and grabbed his hands. "Jason, you're asking the wrong question. The question you should be asking is 'what if there is a curse?'" Katie moved one of Jason's hands to her stomach. "What if there's even a one percent chance this curse could be real? This baby could be a girl, Jason, and we'd only get twenty-five years with her. Is that enough for you? Could you really just sit and wait and hope that four generations of women dying at twenty five is a coincidence of cosmic proportions?"

"No. No, I couldn't just wait." Jason looked from his wife's face to his hand on her still flat stomach and blew out a breath, his honey brown eyes serious. "So, we go to Tranquil Heights, we find out everything we can, and we break the curse."

"We?"

"We."

FIVE

TRANQUIL HEIGHTS PREPARATORY ACADEMY sat on forty acres an hour north of Seattle. It comprised of two stately old brick buildings covered in vines, and Katie was pleased to visit during the spring when those vines were decorated in small pink flowers. The grounds were well manicured, with topiary trees lining the large, round driveway that swept in front of the primary building. She'd been informed to take the smaller drive to the left of the principal building to a large parking lot strategically hidden behind the secondary building.

Katie observed the teenage girls in the courtyard between the buildings as Jason slowly followed the driveway. Just as she had at home, the girls here appeared to be enjoying the return of the sun to western Washington. Many of them had their study books open on blankets laid down on the plush green lawn. Some had taken to a far corner with lacrosse equipment, and others were sunning themselves with no apparent distractions.

The first thing Katie noticed as she exited her vehicle was the quiet. Of course, she could hear the chatter and laughter of the students, but otherwise it was eerily quiet. In the city, one spent little time listening to birds chirping or the rustling of the trees as a gentle breeze tickled their leaves. Katie had grown used to a deluge of city sounds that had become the constant background hum of her life.

"It's quiet here." Jason said. He drew in a deep breath of air and blew it out with a contented sigh. What little length his short, dark brown hair had on top shifted in the gentle breeze. "And the air is fresher. Everything just feels a bit purer here, doesn't it?"

"It does," Katie agreed.

"Maybe it's time to think about moving out of the city. I'd love to have a yard where we could build a swing set for the kids. And imagine putting kids down for a nap without the cacophony of sirens and traffic?" Jason said it casually as he pulled the duffel bags from the trunk. Katie knew his casual tone was a farce.

They'd gone rounds about moving out of the city, though always before Jason had been firmly planted in the "stay in the city" camp. His change of heart surprised and elated her.

"It's amazing. The only noises here are buzzing bees and the wind in the trees. It's all so perfectly... well... tranquil. I guess that's why they call it Tranquil Heights," Katie said, a slight blush building in her cheeks and the beginning of an awkward laugh caught in her throat.

The appearance of a smartly dressed middle-aged woman interrupted the quietude. She had blonde hair pulled back into a high, tight bun, not a flyway baby hair in sight. Katie ran her fingers through her soft waves, cursing the humidity that caused her baby hairs to become a constant halo of frizz around her face.

"You must be Katie and Jason Edgecomb," the woman said as she reached a hand out to each of them. "I'm Valerie Denman, Head Teacher here at Tranquil Heights Preparatory Academy." Her severity lessened with her smile, and Katie reassessed her age as they shook hands. Valerie Denman was likely in her mid-thirties but carried herself with a seriousness that made her seem much older.

"It's so nice to meet you. Thank you, truly, for letting us come out and do some research about my family." Katie smoothed her hands down her floral cotton dress. She couldn't help but note, as she had at the birthday party, how a job really dictated your fashion. Valerie Denman's tailored pantsuit screamed authority figure. Her appearance left no doubt who was in charge of the Academy. Katie dressed precisely how you'd expect a pre-school teacher to dress: in bright colors printed on easily washable fabric that could be thrown in a dryer to release the wrinkles.

"Of course. We are always happy to host those who are interested in the history of Tranquil Heights. In fact, we currently have a visiting doctoral candidate staying with us while she works on her thesis." Valerie led Katie and Jason down the walkway through the courtyard, greeting students with a fondness that Katie recognized as the hallmark of a good educator. "Unfortunately, I have a meeting starting in about fifteen minutes, so I can't give you the grand tour. I'll drop you off in the museum and the manager will take it from there."

They followed Valerie through the front door of the secondary building, noting the name on the door, "Covington Hall." High ceilings and gleaming original tile work greeted them in the large antechamber. The owners of the Preparatory Academy had spared no costs in the painstaking restoration of the buildings, but Katie still felt her jaw drop as she took in the glory of the historical architecture.

"Wow," Jason said, voice barely above a whisper.

"You took the words right out of my mouth," Katie replied, slowly turning in place to look at the entire room.

"It is glorious, isn't it?" Valerie said from her position at the door on the right. "I never get tired of working here because everything is just so beautiful." She opened the door and gestured to it with her opposite hand. "Shall we?"

Katie felt her face grow hot as she ducked her head and half-skipped toward the door. Jason grabbed her hand as she crossed into the next room, pulling her back to slow her down. His eyes twinkled with good humor and love as he squeezed her hand. Katie breathed deeply and smiled at him, soothed and reminded that there was no need to be embarrassed simply because she'd been overcome by the beauty of the building.

A young woman stepped out from behind a counter to the right. She dressed professionally, in slacks and blouse, but gave off a youthful air with a loud print and accessories. Her skin was a pale, golden brown, dotted with deep red freckles. Tight auburn curls were cropped close to her head, leaving her high cheekbones and powerful jaw on prominent display. She locked a startling pair of pale green eyes on Katie and Jason, and the smile she gave them added a friendly sheen to those stunning eyes.

"Jason and Katie Edgecomb, this is Darla Newkirk. She's our manager here at the Tranquil Heights Museum. She'll be your guide while you research your family. As I said, I have a meeting, and I really must be going now. It was nice to meet you both." Valerie nodded respectfully to the three of them before pivoting on her heel and exiting the building.

"I'm so glad to meet you, and I'm excited to help you with your research." Darla had a good, solid handshake and a singsong voice that Katie found soothing. "Valerie tells me you had a family member that worked here when this was still a hospital?"

"Yes, my great-great-grandmother worked here for over thirty years." Katie said.

"Wow. That's amazing. She probably could have told some interesting stories about this place after that many years. The firsthand accounts of people who worked and stayed here are some of my favorite bits of history about Tranquil Heights." Darla's eyes were alight with excitement. Katie could tell that Darla loved the history of Tranquil Heights the same way Katie loved Paint Fridays.

"Something tells me we're incredibly lucky to have you as a resource," Katie said.

Darla's cheeks flushed red with pleasure, and her

smile grew wider. "I'm glad you think so. I can't wait to help you with this." Darla walked back around the counter and reached under it., emerging with a key attached toa large leather keyring stamped with the number 302. "I have to close the museum down for lunch since I'm the only one working. So, I thought I'd show you to your room, and we could get started after lunch, if that's okay?"

SIX

THEIR ROOM WAS IN THE PRIMARY BUILDING, Cumberland Hall. They'd been placed in a wing locked off and separated from the rest of the building. Darla had explained that this wing was for visiting professors or researchers like themselves. The rest of the building housed the students, plus the cafeteria and rec room.

The room was stately, ornately decorated to match the crown molding and gilded fireplace original to the building. The window looked out onto the courtyard where the students were packing up their things in preparation for the afternoon's lessons.

Jason wrapped his arms around Katie as she

watched the students migrate toward Covington Hall. "How incredibly lucky are these girls to study here?" he said, chin resting on the top of Katie's head.

"Pretty lucky. But you know my mixed feelings about private school." Katie turned in Jason's arms and took a step backwards so she could look at him without craning her neck.

"I know. I don't really even disagree with you. Why should some people have the chance at a better education just because their parents have money? We should give students an equal footing."

"Or even putting kids from lower socio-economic homes in private schools, giving the kids who actually need a leg up, the leg up."

Jason smiled down at Katie and kissed her forehead. This was a conversation they'd had many times. Katie sometimes felt that she was lending to an inequitable educational society because she worked for an "elite" private preschool. Every time she brought this up, Jason calmly asked her where else she intended to teach since there were no public preschools in their area. He was, of course, right. Katie hated it when he was right.

"Come on. We should go meet back up with Darla now. We have work to do, Mr. Edgecomb."

"Aye-aye, Captain Katie." Jason saluted his

wife, then marched to the door and held it open for her.

They walked into Covington Hall just as the bell was ringing and the last few stragglers were scrambling up the stairs, struggling to keep hold of their books. Darla waited for them at the main entrance of the museum. "How much do you know about Tranquil Heights?" she asked as she opened the door for them and ushered them inside.

"Not much, honestly. I remember the newspaper articles in the early 2000s saying the land had been purchased and the new owners intended to return the grounds and buildings to their former glory and open a private school. I know this had been a mental hospital until 1979 when it closed. And then it sat empty until the current owners bought it," Katie listed what she knew as Darla nodded along.

"You've got just the tip of the iceberg there. I think we should start at the beginning." Darla practically skipped as she led Katie and Jason to a wall with old sepia toned photos. The photos showed Tranquil Heights in various stages of construction until the last photo depicted the two buildings—large brick affairs with multiple half-hexagonal outcroppings running across the front of each façade—much the same as they stood today. Large windows graced all three floors, flooding the buildings with natural light.

The Edgecombs followed Darla as she explained the history. "Tranquil Heights started life as a sanitarium in 1910," she explained as she pointed to the first photo that contained people. The grainy sepia figures sat in wheelchairs, blankets spread over their laps. "Tuberculosis was the largest cause of death in the Seattle area and doctors thought that crisp, fresh air could treat tuberculosis, so a real estate magnate and contractor worked together to build and open Tranquil Heights. It offered hope to the wealthy and connected in Seattle, being the premiere private pay sanitarium in the area."

Darla moved towards a set of interior photos. "The primary building, now called Cumberland Hall, had been home to the residents. The rooms were large, ornately decorated and furnished, and private."

Jason leaned in to get a closer look at the photos, eyes shifting quickly. "Must have been something else to stay here," he said.

"It was lavish, for sure," Darla replied, smiling ruefully. "But no one was exactly happy to be here, you know, since they were sick?"

Jason nodded, grinning sheepishly.

"The other building housed the staff," Darla continued, this time pointing out interior photos that displayed rooms with less in them, though they were still large and well appointed. "In 1932, in response to the decreasing need for private pay sanitariums, Tranquil Heights converted to a hospital for wayward girls and women. It was still a private pay facility and became home to the wealthy elite's dirty little secrets. Here, families would bring their wives, daughters, and sisters to live and "recover" from a variety of ailments, from made-up issues like hysteria"—Darla caught Katie's eye and the two exchanged an eye roll—"to actual mental conditions that hadn't yet been named. Only the ten largest rooms remained private, while the other fifty patient rooms became shared rooms. Due to the increase in patients, the hospital enjoyed a vast increase in profit margins and could landscape more of the grounds, building the large, grassy courtyard dotted with ponds and gazebos that between the two buildings." Darla stopped in front a set of black and white photos, each one displaying a new addition to the grounds.

"And then, in 1953, the hospital once again transformed itself, this time into a full-fledged mental hospital, though it remained private pay. The capacity remained the same, but the hospital now accepted men. The hospital served as an example of luxurious private pay, moral treatment care until the mid-sixties," Darla put air quotes around the words "moral treatment."

"In the sixties, the mental health system was deinstitutionalized and the large state institutions started to close their door. Tranquil Heights limped along by upping the room capacity. They marketed the grounds as a place to "relax and rejuvenate" in order to continue to attract the wealthy families of the mentally ill. Unfortunately, because the hospital was struggling financially, the management didn't hire more staff, and the standard of care fell dramatically," Darla stopped in front of a series of framed newspaper articles about the facility. The dates ranged from the late sixties to late seventies and the headlines portrayed a nightmare. *Not So Tranquil Heights* read one, accompanied by a photo of an overstuffed recreation room. *Prominent Community Members Call for Closure of "Barbaric" Mental Institution* claimed another, the photo showing filthy patients lying or sitting on the hard tile floor. "Tranquil Heights ultimately closed in 1979 after nearly a decade of decreasing demand and increasing public outcry at the way patients were treated.

"The grounds spent the next twenty-three years empty and decaying, attracting vagrants, partying teenagers, and various wildlife. It gained a reputation for being haunted and enjoyed visits from spooky-enthused tourists and amateur ghost hunters. In 2003, the forty-acre lot was sold for far less than its worth, and renovations on the property immediately began returning Tranquil Heights to her former glory," Darla finished and stood in front of a large full color photo of the grounds as they stood today.

"I wish I could have seen the grounds when they were abandoned," Katie said, drifting back over to the photos of the overgrown and graffitied buildings.

"Me too," replied Darla. "I love that kind of spooky stuff, you know?" Katie smiled at Darla and nodded.

"When exactly did your great-great-grandmother work here?" Darla asked after a long moment of silence as they'd stared at the old photos together.

"She started in 1934 and retired in 1967," Katie replied. Her mind wandered through the history and connected the dots about what kind of patients her great-great-grandmother had seen.

"Okay, so post sanitarium. I will say that the hospital kept incredible records and we are so lucky as a museum to have access to many of them. What was her name?"

"Wilhelmina Darrington."

"Oh!" Darla let out a crow of excited laughter, face alight with knowledge and recognition. She grabbed Katie's hand and pulled her to the middle of the room where a weathered, leather-bound journal sat open beneath a protective plastic barrier. A plaque explained that the box was temperature and moisture controlled to preserve the journal. Beneath that, in bold letters, it said: *Journal of Wilhelmina Darrington, Nurse at Tranquil Heights 1934-35.* Katie felt her jaw drop and her eyes go wide.

Jason's face reflected her pleased shock. "What are the odds, eh, Katie?" he said, one eyebrow cocked and a graceful shrug lifting his shoulders.

"It gets better," Darla said, pointing to the plaque again. "This journal was found in the floorboards of the room you're staying in!"

"What are the odds, indeed?" Katie asked.

"Curiouser and curiouser," Jason said, a glint of humor in his eyes. Katie knew Jason saw this as one heck of a coincidence, and that was it. Katie wanted to believe the same. A cool trickle of sweat slid down her spine, tickling the small, raised hairs. Coincidences were stacking on top of coincidences, and Katie felt as though Tranquil Heights had been waiting for her all these years.

"Darla, do you have copies of the journal that I could read?" she asked, voice shaking.

"Yes. Every record found was scanned and digitized to help preserve the history. Let me just print you off a copy." Darla was clearly pleased that Katie's research had started off with such a boon, and she hummed happily to herself as a printer worked behind her.

Katie and Jason returned to their room, the paper copy of her great-great-grandmother's journal still hot in her hands. Jason sat at the desk in one corner of the room and opened his laptop to answer some work emails, allowing Katie some time to absorb the shock of the day. Katie settled into a comfy chintz armchair under a lamp and began reading.

SEVEN

TRANQUIL HEIGHTS
DECEMBER 1934

WILHELMINA DARRINGTON SMILED as she pulled into work for her swing shift. It was December 14th, and the maintenance crew had spent the day putting up the Christmas decorations. The buildings and trees lining the driveway were outlined with strings of multi-colored lights. Large red ribbons graced every window, and fresh green wreathes hung from every exterior door.

She had spent the previous day with her husband, Bradley, and two-year-old daughter, Eleanor, decorating their own home. Though they couldn't afford anything so lavish as Tranquil Heights, their home was lit up with modest lights, and gleaming tinsel winked at them from the tree in the corner of their living room. Wilhelmina Darrington loved Christmas. The lights and cheery decorations brought so much joy into life, just when it was needed most in the long, chilly nights of Washington's winter.

Wilhelmina's white shoes squeaked on the tile flooring despite having been wiped on the mats lain at the service entrance to the primary building. A young girl at the nurse's station looked up as Wilhelmina rounded the corner, a bright smile lighting up her face. She was lining the nurse's station with so much gold and silver tinsel that Wilhelmina almost couldn't see the wood of the station.

"Violet, I see they've cut you loose with the box of Christmas decorations." Wilhelmina was fond of Violet, who was only fifteen and volunteering at Tranquil Heights. She was exceedingly smart and listened closely to any direction she was given. Wilhelmina was certain she'd make an excellent nurse someday.

"This is probably the best assignment I've ever been given," Violet replied with a giggle. "Do you think it would be too much if I hung ornaments from the tinsel?" She held an ornament out at arm's reach, with one eye closed and the tip of her tongue just poking out from between her lips.

"Of course it would be too much, Violet, but why on earth should that stop you?" Wilhelmina picked up an ornament and hung it from one of the many strands of tinsel.

The front door to the primary building opened as Wilhelmina and Violet debated the correct number of ornaments to make the decorations "too much" but not "too far." A male orderly was escorting a young woman into the building. His elbow held out to her as though he were her date to the prom.

Wilhelmina's gaze slid down the woman's body and stopped at the slight bump that stretched her skirt tight across her stomach. Wilhelmina and Violet smiled at the woman as she walked past the nurse's station. The patients may not have been here voluntarily, but this was still a premiere private pay facility, and the patients were to be treated as guests.

"That's the third one in three months," Violet said, shaking her head. "Justin told me the other two came with checks signed by the same person."

"You and the orderlies would do well to remember not to gossip about our guests. Their situations are none of our business outside of the bare minimum we need to know to care for them."

Wilhelmina and Violet returned to decorating in

silence, blush gracing Violet's cheeks. Though Wilhelmina would say nothing, she knew for a fact that the first two women to arrive pregnant out of wedlock were indeed here under the same payor, a prominent businessman, simply cleaning up the messes of his philandering young son. She sniffed to herself. It seemed unfair to her that those women were shut up here out of the public eye to have and give up their babies while the father continued to party about town.

Wilhelmina was the head nurse on the evening shift and was expected to take part in new patient enrollments. She sat in Dr. Covington's large office in a comfortable armchair. Justin Chase, the orderly with the gift of gab, sat in the chair next to her with a notepad and pen in the ready positions.

"New patient is twenty-four-year-old female Natalie Arthur. Natalie presents as four months pregnant, expected due date is May 6, 1935. Natalie is a maid for the Cumberland family," Dr. Covington said, pacing behind his desk.

Justin's eyes grew very round, and he stared resolutely at the notepad in front of him. Wilhelmina was more in control of her facial expressions, but she felt the same shock Justin was displaying. State Senator Cumberland was very popular in the Capitol. Speculators thought it likely that Governor

Abbot would be forced to retire soon due to illness and Senator Cumberland was on the short list to replace him. Infidelity, and a child borne out of it, was a surefire way to lose the good favor he carried in the political circles.

"I will remind you that discretion is of utmost importance here at Tranquil Heights. The families of our patients pay a good deal of money to keep their family issues out of the limelight." Dr. Covington stopped pacing and took a moment to make serious eye contact with both Wilhelmina and Justin.

Tranquil Heights was a private pay center for "wayward girls and women." Sometimes wayward meant those with true mental health needs who could benefit from the help of the doctors on staff. Most of the time wayward meant unruly, strong headed, or pregnant out of wedlock. Tranquil Heights was a place where a person could lock away their "embarrassing" female family members, or powerful men could hide their indiscretions. Wilhelmina thought it was a stretch to call the Cumberlands Natalie Arthur's "family," but she knew appearances meant a lot to the people who used Tranquil Heights.

She would rather work in a proper hospital where she was helping those in genuine need, but the private pay nature of Tranquil Heights benefited her. Working at Tranquil Heights paid significantly more than working in a public hospital, and with a two year old, she couldn't afford to have her morals come before her paycheck. Her husband worked an early morning shift in a factory, so he was home about an hour before Wilhelmina left for work. One of her parents always cared for their daughter, Eleanor, and the Darringtons needn't worry about the cost of childcare. Frankly, so many people were out of work and homeless that Wilhelmina and Bradley Darrington were lucky to have jobs at all, let alone one that paid like Tranquil Heights.

"Nurse Darrington, will you please go see that Ms. Arthur is settled and happy with her accommodations?"

Wilhelmina made her way to the third floor, where the private rooms were. The Cumberlands had spared no expense in hiding this indiscretion. Many of the wealthy families assumed that if you spoiled the girl, she'd keep her mouth shut. Wilhelmina knew for a fact that most of them would have been happy to keep their mouths shut if they would have just been allowed to move away and live their own lives rather than being locked away in the world's most comfortable prison.

Wilhelmina knocked on the door to room 302 and only entered once she'd heard a stuffy voice say "come in." The appearance of privacy was also very important in Tranquil Heights. The staff wanted the patients to feel as though they were on a lavish retreat rather than involuntarily admitted to a hospital.

Natalie Arthur was a striking young woman. Her face was round and soft, almost cherubic. Her blue eyes were clear and crisp like a mountain lake. Wilhelmina pretended not to notice the sparkle of tears and red splotches on her face. Natalie's thick, luxurious hair that sat lightly upon her shoulders in a loose wave was the type of blonde that movie stars paid a lot of money for. It looked as though it had been spun from gold and carried the depth of natural high and low lights.

"Ms. Arthur, I'm Nurse Darrington. I work the evening shift here so you'll see me in the late afternoons and at dinner Thursday through Monday. Dinner is held in the formal dining room on the first floor at six p.m. every day, and we expect that you dress for it." Natalie nodded silently in response, blotting gently at her nose with a plain cotton handkerchief. "I trust you find your accommodations to your liking?"

Natalie looked at Wilhelmina as though she could see straight through to her soul. Her face had hardened with anger, and the cherubic quality disappeared. Wilhelmina felt sure that Natalie Arthur was not just a pretty face; there was a weight of intelligence in the young woman's eyes, a shrewdness that made her seem more than four years older than Wilhelmina. Nathalie Arthur had learned lessons the hard way and had faced challenges that Wilhelmina Darrington could never even have imagined.

"Tranquil Heights is very beautiful, Nurse Darrington. It ought to be with how much Mr. Cumberland is paying for it. The accommodations are lavish, as they should be. The furniture is comfortable, the view exquisite, and I'm certain the food will be divine. The accommodations are exactly to Mr. Cumberland's liking, Nurse Darrington. But not to mine. I don't want to be here at all. It doesn't matter how beautiful it is, or how great the food is, or how well I'm pampered. I do not choose to be here. I would never choose to be here. So no, Nurse Darrington, these accommodations are *not* to my liking." Natalie's voice was filled with venom and she resolutely turned away from Wilhelmina, who could only back out of the room.

Wilhelmina stood in the hallway outside of room 302, her back to the door, hand still on the knob. Natalie Arthur had been the first patient to vocalize the issues that Wilhelmina herself had with

Tranquil Heights. The interaction shook her, and she hoped she wouldn't have to spend much time with their newest patient. She just didn't have it in her to sympathize so very much with one of Tranquil Heights' wayward women.

EIGHT

WILHELMINA WATCHED THREE PREGNANT WOMEN at a small table lean closer together, lips moving in a blur between giggles. She narrowed her eyes, suspicious of what would come of that conversation and wishing she could hear them over the Christmas music on the gramophone. It was Christmas Eve and Tranquil Heights' three pregnant young women had bonded over the last ten days.

Beatrice Satler and Alice Pullman were both only nineteen and found themselves at Tranquil Heights not only for the same reason, but because of the same wild young man. Alice was still naïve enough to believe that Connor Hatfield loved her and would change his mind and she'd be swept away to live happily ever after. She came from an excellent family and had catered to every whim of Connor's under the belief that he would ask for her hand in marriage any day.

Meanwhile, Connor had also been seeing Beatrice and who knew how many other women. Beatrice had lived a harder life and worked as a waitress at a club he frequented. She knew full well what she was getting into with Connor and had no plans to marry him. She just believed that if Connor could sow his wild oats, so could she.

The relative youth of Beatrice and Alice made Natalie the oldest at her ripe age of twenty four. Wilhelmina was sure it wasn't just Natalie's five more years on the planet that drew Beatrice and Alice to her. There was a fierce magnetism to Natalie that made her a natural leader, made her someone people wanted to be with. Wilhelmina had avoided private interactions with Natalie since that first night, but she couldn't seem to stop herself from observing the young woman from a comfortable distance.

Natalie turned to look at Wilhelmina, and it was like a storm cloud moved overhead, blocking the sun but filling the air where Wilhelmina stood with a hot pressure. This was, of course, impossible since they were inside the dining room. Wilhelmina shuddered, goosebumps cropping up on her arms under her white sweater. The right side of Natalie's face lifted just slightly, and Wilhelmina would have sworn that Natalie knew what she was feeling if she hadn't been a more sensible woman.

Despite Wilhelmina's suspicions, Tranquil Heights' Christmas Eve dinner went on without a hiccup or disruption from its three merry mistresses. She watched as the patients wandered out of the dining room, off to their individual rooms or the common room for the rest of the evening, and the tight knot in her stomach relaxed by millimeters.

She conducted her nightly checks of the medical wings, ensuring that everything was locked up and inaccessible to the wandering rogue patient. Though many of the patients were like Beatrice, Alice, and Natalie—women who didn't conform to the standards of the society outside the walls of Tranquil Heights— some of them needed proper care for legitimate mental health conditions. It wouldn't do for the medical equipment or medications to be easily accessible to those who might use them to hurt themselves.

Wilhelmina tugged on the doors of the locked medication cabinets and paused when she heard a faint hissing sound from down the hallway. She strained her ears, waiting for the sound to happen again. This time, she heard a slight squeak, as though the toe of a shoe had caught on the gleaming tile floors.

It wasn't uncommon for patients to be up past ten p.m., but they rarely fretted about making noise, and Wilhelmina got the distinct feeling that whoever was making the noise intended to sneak.

Wilhelmina moved into the hallway cautiously, a cool sweat breaking out across her body. There was a flickering light coming from under the door at the end of the hall. Wilhelmina's shoulders sagged, and she let out a shaky breath as she shook her head at her own silliness. The door at the end of the hallway was the service entrance to the common room where patients could use the television set, listen to the radio, or play games. Wilhelmina wiped her clammy hands on her skirt as she walked down the hallway, intent to check on the person in the common room.

Three sets of eyes greeted her when she opened the door. One set, the color of a dark honey in the sun, belonged to Beatrice. Another, a medium brown flecked with green like newly growing flower beds, belonged to Alice. The last pair, a blue so pale and bright it looked like ice, is what stopped Wilhelmina in her tracks. It was almost painful for Wilhelmina to tear her gaze away from Natalie's.

Beatrice, Alice, and Natalie were sitting in a close circle, hands held palm up, three candles flickering on a plate on the floor between them. The air in the room seemed thick, like a summer day when the humidity was high and it felt as though you were pushing through a weighty curtain with every move.

Wilhelmina didn't understand why, but cold tendrils of fear gripped her heart, and she struggled to swallow past the scream that lodged itself in her throat.

NINE

KATIE'S EYES BURNED WITH TIREDNESS and she rubbed at them as she put down the loose sheets of paper. Her great-great-grandmother had been rather verbose, and she'd made it through only ten days out of the months' worth of journal entries. So far all she'd learned was that Wilhelmina Darrington loved Christmas and was a feminist in her time. Those were both wonderful things to know about a long past relative, but not so important to Katie's goal of uncovering the curse.

She slid the window down and latched it, sparing a quick glance at Jason to ensure she didn't wake him. She turned off the reading lamp and, with a sigh, Katie crawled into bed and said a silent prayer that tomorrow she would find out something more. She drifted off to sleep, thinking of twinkling Christmas lights, flickering candles, and an overarching sense of existential dread.

Katie woke with a start. She blinked wearily at the clock on the nightstand, the red lines glowing 11:32pm. She'd only been asleep for half an hour and the warm covers were threatening to pull her back under, but she had a tingle at the back of her neck that told her something had woken her up. Katie's eyes quickly traced the unfamiliar room, and as far as she could tell, nothing was out of place.

A slight fluttering from Jason's side of the room caught her attention, and she gently got out of bed and padded across the room. The sheer curtains over the window danced lazily in the cool breeze. Goosebumps popped up over her bare arms, the tiny hairs standing at attention, saluting the brisk spring night. She slid the window closed and latched it, shivering as she made her way back to the warm covers.

Just as she pulled back the corner of the blankets, she heard a distinct creaking noise from the other side of the room. Her eyes strained in the darkness, trying to catch any glimpse of movement. A shudder ran through Katie and hard goosebumps sprang up almost painfully. Her hand clenched the blanket as though she would pull it up over her head out of reflex. The monsters can't get you when you're under the blankets.

Katie groped blindly for the bedside lamp and twisted the knob as soon as her fingers felt it. The small lamp cast the room in deep shadows, but nothing was out of place. Jason groaned as he sat up, making Katie jump.

"Hey, you okay?" Jason crawled across the bed to her. When he drew even with her, he rose on his knees and grabbed her chin. "You look pale. Are you sick?"

"I thought... I..." Katie swallowed heavily and glanced down at her hand, blanket still clutched tightly in fingers that had gone white. She dropped the blanket and flexed her hand, noting the ache and faint tremor that had set in.

"Katelyn." Jason's voice was harsh and abrupt. Katie blinked into his eyes. He never used her full name unless something was wrong. He raised his eyebrows at her, a silent reminder that he was waiting for the answer to a question.

"Right. Sorry. I just... something woke me up. I'm not even sure what. But I swear I heard something move." She glanced over towards the window as if expecting to finally see the thing that made the phantom noise.

"What exactly did you hear?" he asked as he set both hands on Katie's upper arms, rubbing them in a slow and comforting pattern. Jason's voice was calm and practical. He was a good man in a crisis and always countered Katie's emotional reactions with logic. It was both a blessing and infuriating.

"A creak, over by the window." Katie pointed with her chin.

Jason walked over to that side of the bed, and just as he made it to the window, the floorboards protested with a high whine. "Was it that? Is that what you heard?"

"Yes," Katie whispered. She hugged her arms tightly to her chest, trying to chase away the cold dread that seemed to have seeped into her bones.

Jason moved around the room cautiously, turning on all the lights. He checked behind every curtain, in the closet, in the bathroom, and under the bed. There was no one in the room but the two of them. He wrapped Katie in his arms, and she melted into the warmth of him.

"It's an old building, Katie," Jason murmured into her hair. "Old buildings settle and make weird noises. There's definitely no one in here, so that's probably what you heard."

"Being silly," Katie replied, nodding rapidly. Now that the room was brightly lit and Jason was awake, she realized that she'd let her own imagination run away with her. "The last thing I read in my great-

great-grandmother's journal was that she discovered three patients doing... I don't know. I guess some kind of ritual, maybe. It scared her, and I think I let it spook me."

"It's not silly. It's all a bit spooky, isn't it? The whole reason we're even here?"

"You know this is why I love you, right?"

"Among many, many other things," Jason teased. "Come on, let's go back to bed. There are no monsters under the bed tonight."

Katie turned off the lamp and let Jason pull her down into bed. She snuggled tight against him, holding his arm to her chest like her favorite teddy bear.

"Jason?"

"Hmm?"

"Did you get up to open the window?"

"No, it was open when I went to sleep."

Katie lay awake for a long time, straining to hear any sign of movement in the room, eyes squeezed tightly shut. After an hour of hearing nothing but the sound of Jason's even breathing, sleep finally dragged her under.

TEN

KATIE AND JASON SAT AT A TABLE in the cafeteria, sipping coffee. The stack of journal pages lay face down on the table next to Katie. She was on her third cup of coffee, the second hour at the table, and still hadn't flipped them over. She stared at them, a crease forming between her eyes, foot bobbing up and down impatiently.

"Are you going to tell me what was in the journal that bothered you?" Jason asked, peering at her from over his laptop.

Darla appeared, saving Katie from having to tell him about the journal. She was like a hurricane of effervescent happiness, dressed in a canary yellow dress and carrying a sparkly pink tumbler.

"Hello, Edgecombs! Mind if I join you?" Darla didn't wait for an answer before pulling out a chair and plopping down unceremoniously. "How far did you make it in the journal?" she asked, pointing to the stack of papers.

"Not as far as I would have thought," Katie admitted.

Darla laughed. "Yeah, I got the feeling that Wilhelmina was quite a talker," she said, nodding.

"You've read the journal?" Katie asked, eyes intent on Darla's face.

"Oh, yeah. Anything that's public record about this place, I've read."

"What is your connection to this place?"

"Oh, I graduated three years ago from the Academy. I fell in love with the grounds and the history. I'm studying history at U-Dub."

"You stayed close for college. I would have thought students from Tranquil Heights would have their pick of schools, including Ivy League," Jason interjected. Katie stifled a smile. Jason's ambition paralleled Liz's, and neither of them could understand someone not leaping at the best opportunity.

"Oh, I had my pick. They accepted me at Harvard, Yale, and Stanford," Darla said with the air of nonchalance of someone talking about which grocery store they preferred. "I just couldn't bring myself to leave this place."

"Why the attachment? What's so special about this place?" Jason asked.

"Haven't you felt it? This place is alive. She has a story to tell, and no one's listening to her. Except me." Darla glanced at Jason, but locked eyes with Katie.

Jason raised his eyebrows but kept his comments to himself and returned his attention to his laptop. Katie was staring at Darla as though the young woman had sprouted a second head. She understood what Darla meant. She had the distinct sense that Tranquil Heights had been waiting for her and was ready to spill all its secrets at her feet if she'd let it.

"What do you make of Beatrice, Alice, and Natalie in the common room? That's where I stopped reading last night," Katie said.

Darla gave her a knowing smile. "Ah. Yes, that is a very interesting event. But I will not tell you what I think until you've read further."

"It's not a new novel, Darla. You aren't going to spoil the story for me."

"Some things you just need to learn for yourself," Darla replied with a shrug. "I do have something I'd like to show you in the museum, if you're interested?"

Katie looked at the copied pages on the table. She really did not want to read again. Something about the sun outside the large dining room windows made it seem inappropriate to the read the words of the dead.

She looked up at Jason's face over his laptop and found him watching her.

"Do you want me to go with you?" he asked.

"I always want you with me," she replied. The answer was a reflex, something they said to each other automatically in response to that question.

"This is your project. You haven't told me yet what's in those pages, and I don't want to push you on it. I'm here to be as involved as you want or need me to be."

"Then you should come to the museum with us."

"Then it's settled," Darla said with a clap of her hands. She bounced out of her chair and held a hand out to Katie. "I can't wait to show you what I've found."

.   .   .

What Darla had found cluttered the large desk at the entry of the museum. Dozens of black and white photos were spread out, interspersed with old newspaper clippings.

"I started digging through the image archives after you left yesterday. And I found these photos from the space of time that Wilhelmina worked here." Darla started pushing photos towards Katie and Jason.

Many of the photos showed patients taking part in fun activities, a sort of advertisement for the luxury of getting "help" from Tranquil Heights. Katie noticed the edge of a photo that looked like the dining room and moved it out from under a newspaper article about the facility. In it, three young women sat around a table. They were smiling but somehow conveyed a seriousness in their proper posture. It felt like they were part of an exclusive club and the photographer, and by extension Katie, was not welcome to join.

The woman in the middle rested her hand on a pregnant belly protectively. There was a gentleness in her, a jovial quirk to her lips, that made her less serious than the other two. Katie's eyes quickly flicked to the midsections of the other two women, both of whom were sporting their own smaller bumps. The woman on the right was very light. Her hair was so blonde it reflected the light in the room, and her eyes took on that unsettling white quality that light blue eyes do in black and white photos. The woman on the left was darker. She had high cheekbones, hair that may have been dark brown or black, and thick eyebrows. A Christmas tree sat in the corner, the tinsel glinting in the dining room lights. The caption at the bottom of the photo said "Christmas 1934."

"Holy fuck! This is Beatrice, Alice, and Natalie!" Katie said, looking up at Darla in wonder.

"I know. Isn't it amazing? Your great-great-grandmother described them so well, I knew who they were before I even saw the caption."

"This might have been taken just before the... the ritual that Wilhelmina walked in on." Katie said ritual with the upwards lilt of a question.

"Ritual is an apt description," Darla replied, nodding.

"I'm sorry, but what ritual? This is the second time you've mentioned a ritual," Jason interjected, still looking down at the photo of the three women.

Katie quickly gave him the Cliff's Notes version of what Wilhelmina had walked in on, and her description of the atmosphere of the room and the fear she'd felt. Jason kept his face carefully blank while he listened.

"So, what? These three were doing some kind of...spell? Or witchcraft? I mean, that's ridiculous." The words hung in the air, an uncomfortable silence stretching as Katie and Darla locked eyes. "Katie, seriously. Do you think they were like...Wiccans or something?"

"No, Jason. Not Wiccans." Katie finally met Jason's eyes. She saw his skepticism and confusion. Liz had spent her whole life with that same skepticism and Katie had followed suit, staying silent when Liz had scoffed at the ghost stories in Girl Scout campouts.

While Katie had been skeptical of the family's curse and understood Liz's rejection of all things paranormal, she had secretly always felt like some things simply couldn't be explained away by science or logic. This was one of those moments to Katie. She was already re-evaluating something she and Liz had been so sure of. Why not everything else along with it?

"Then what, Katie?"

"Witches. I don't have another word to use. I don't think we're talking about the modern burn some sage, worship in nature interpretation. If I could call them something else, I would. But... I think at the very least Wilhelmina thought these women were witches."

"Okay. I'll accept that. Wilhelmina caught them doing something weird. It gave her the willies." Jason looked like he would like to say more, opened his mouth, appeared to think better of it, and left the conversation where it was.

"You'll find more answers in the journal about these three. Probably more questions, too," Darla said. Katie thought that was a most unhelpful statement. "But I have one more thing to show you."

Darla scanned the photos on the desktop, searching for something in particular. When she found it, she pulled it out, holding it so the back of it faced Katie and Jason. Her eyes were alight with humor and expectation as she turned it around to face them.

The photo contained three women in full nurse's uniforms and a younger girl, maybe a teenager, in a white skirt and blouse without the little hat. The woman standing second to the right was all hard angles. She had high cheekbones, a strong jaw, and her hair pulled back tightly so there was nothing to distract from that familiar bone structure.

"Oh, Liz," Katie said on an exhale. She reached out to the photo as though she'd trace her fingers down the contour of the woman's face.

"This is the nursing staff from 1935," Darla explained, voice hushed. She watched Katie with wary eyes, as if she'd picked up on the other woman's grief. "The second from the right is Wilhelmina Darrington, but I guess you already realized that."

Katie took the photo from Darla, eyes never leaving the woman who looked like her sister. Jason grabbed her other hand, giving it a gentle squeeze. She blinked away tears and called down that part of her that had always connected to Liz. She searched for that spark, that fierceness, and found only silence and emptiness.

ELEVEN

BEATRICE SATLER WAS ANGRY. She moved through Tranquil Heights on a cloud of passionate impatience, ready to vocally accost anyone unfortunate enough to be in her path. Wilhelmina watched as a shy old woman who had mentally stopped developing at the age of ten scurried out of Beatrice's way. Wilhelmina Darrington had had enough of the young woman's unhappiness leaking all over Tranquil Heights. She marched forward and grabbed Beatrice by the elbow, pulling her out of the common room through the service entrance and into a medical room. Even the rooms where patients were seen for various medical and psychological issues were comfortably appointed, and Wilhelmina pointed at the plush couch against the wall.

"Sit," she said brusquely, arms crossed over her chest.

Beatrice opened her mouth to argue, seemed to think better of it, and tossed her body down onto the couch. She stared at a spot on the blank wall as though there were an interesting painting with many layers to inspect there. Wilhelmina noted the tension singing through Beatrice's entire body. It was almost as though the very air around her crackled with the intensity of the young woman's anger.

"You want to tell me why you're walking around here treating everyone like they killed your puppy?" Wilhelmina asked as she took a seat in an armchair across from the couch.

"Come on, Wilhelmina, do you really have to ask?" Beatrice gestured to at her large midsection.

"You're angry because you're pregnant?" A crease appeared between Wilhelmina's eyebrows. "Beatrice, you're almost six months pregnant. You weren't angry last month. Or at least not outwardly like this. What's changed?"

"It's not just that I'm pregnant, Wilhelmina. It's that I'm pregnant and being hidden away here. It's that Connor Hatfield isn't being hidden away even though he's just as responsible for this situation as I am."

"I don't disagree with you."

"And Alice. She loves him, god help her." Beatrice relaxed by inches. "But how many more of us do you think there are? How many more women just didn't bother to tell him they were pregnant because they were smart enough to realize he wouldn't do the honorable thing?"

The heat of Beatrice's anger seemed to fade and a cold bitterness replaced it, raising goosebumps on Wilhelmina's arms. The air took on a heavy quality that reminded her of Christmas Eve, and she took a deep breath in through her nose to quell the inexplicable panic.

"You aren't stupid, Beatrice. And Alice, though idealistic, isn't stupid either. It isn't stupid to expect people to behave in a way that doesn't hurt others."

Beatrice snorted and heaved herself off the couch. Her hand was on the door handle when she looked back and watched Wilhelmina the way a snake might watch a mouse. Wilhelmina focused on keeping her face calm but interested, ready to listen. The silence stretched between them. The only sound was the pulsing of Wilhelmina's heartbeat in her ears, matching the frantic fluttering of the trapped thing in her chest.

"Tranquil Heights Center of Wayward Women

and Girls." Beatrice snorted again. "Do you ever think they call us wayward or hysterical because they know we're powerful?"

"What do you mean?" The whooshing in Wilhelmina's ears was so loud she could barely hear herself talk. Or maybe it was because she'd spoken softly, afraid she knew what the answer was.

"Some of us... there's something special about us. I know you can feel it. I can see the goosebumps, your pulse speeding up in your neck. You try to hide it. But you feel it. And I bet that means you're more like me than you'd like to admit."

A knock came at the door and Wilhelmina jumped so violently that her bones seemed to rattle with the force of it. Beatrice let out a laugh and opened the door to reveal Natalie. Wilhelmina let out a shaky breath and stood up, smoothing her white skirt down her thighs.

"You're nervous," Natalie said as a way of greeting as she entered the room.

"I beg your pardon?" Wilhelmina managed an air of indignation, though she knew full well that she was nervous. More than nervous—frightened.

"You always smooth the front of your skirt over your thighs when you're nervous or upset about something," Natalie said, nodding down at Wilhelmina's hands. Wilhelmina had to fight the urge to smooth her skirt again.

"Did you need something, Natalie?" Wilhelmina had decided that she would focus on her professionalism when dealing with her. She hoped that focus would keep the skin crawling feeling she didn't understand under control.

"I wanted to make sure Beatrice was okay. I saw you take her out of the common room," Natalie said, though she never looked at Wilhelmina. She stared at Beatrice, and Wilhelmina had the strange feeling they were communicating.

Wilhelmina had run from the common room on Christmas Eve, fighting the urge to scream wildly throughout the building. She had spent many nights lying awake, trying to make sense of what she had felt that night. Beatrice, Alice, and Natalie had done nothing to her, except look at her. And she couldn't blame them for that. She would have looked at someone entering the room, too. She did not know what they had been doing, and had no real reason to assume that it was something negative, other than the near insufferable thickness of the air that made Wilhelmina feel like she was drowning.

She couldn't explain why fear marched over her skin like ants, or why her veins seemed to fill with ice every time she met Natalie's eyes. *Do you ever think they call us wayward or hysterical because they know we're powerful?* Is that what it was? Did the room fill near to choking with power?

Looking at Natalie and Beatrice at that moment, Wilhelmina was sure that what she felt in that room was their power. She just didn't understand how they did it.

"Beatrice was so angry and scaring the other patients. I wanted to make sure she was okay, too," Wilhelmina said. She wanted desperately to leave the room, but Natalie was standing in front of the door.

"Beatrice is angry because what she wants isn't happening," Natalie stated. She casually leaned against the closed door and fixed her gaze on the nurse.

"What do you want, Beatrice?" Wilhelmina asked, eyes flicking between her and Natalie. She felt like a small prey animal caught between two predators. Take her eyes off of them, for even a moment, and it was all over.

"To not be in this situation. I don't want to be here. I don't want to be pregnant." Beatrice's voice had shifted down an octave, gruff with her anger. It took on a graveled quality that reminded Wilhelmina of a growl.

"I can understand that." Wilhelmina licked her lips, tasting the salt of the sweat that had broken out across her upper lip. "I don't think anyone would want to be in your situation, Beatrice."

"I suppose you're right." Beatrice stepped up next to Natalie, gaze fixed on her, and back to Wilhelmina. "But then, most people couldn't do anything about it either." She jerked open the door and walked into the hallway, her roiling anger hot on her heels.

Wilhelmina started at the section of hallway just outside of the door, jaw fallen open and the confused replay of Beatrice's words bouncing around her mind.

"What did she mean? She can't do anything about it either. None of us can." Wilhelmina's voice came out higher pitched than she would have liked, a trace of desperation leaking into it.

"Life has a way of balancing itself out, Wilhelmina," Natalie said as she walked out the door, leaving Wilhelmina in a suddenly cold, empty, and powerless room.

TWELVE

KATIE LAY AWAKE IN THE DARK, listening to Jason's even breathing, brain fixated on Beatrice Satler and the unfair standard she was held to as a woman. Wilhelmina had been afraid of Beatrice, had described things that didn't seem possible. Katie was plagued with confusion and self-doubt. The events of the past few weeks had led her to question everything she thought she knew. She and Liz had been so certain that the family curse wasn't real. Now, Katie wasn't sure about anything, except for the fact that she was in over her head.

Liz had always taken charge, done the research, made the decisions. Katie was loyal to a fault and would have followed Liz to the ends of the earth, so sure was she of her sister's intelligence and good intentions. But now she was cast adrift, floating in an ocean of despair and confusion without the life preserver that was Liz.

She tried desperately to think of what Liz would tell her in this situation and she just kept wrapping back around to the term "crazy." Liz would say that Wilhelmina was just as crazy as the rest of their family. Katie couldn't accept that answer because that would mean she was living in her family's crazy town, population: three. Katie sighed and glanced at her watch. 11:32pm and no hope of sleep in sight.

A quiet creak distracted Katie from her circling thoughts and she stilled under the covers, breath caught in her throat, tension singing down the arm that still held her watch in front of her face. There was a creak again, followed by a clicking noise that sounded deafening to Katie in the otherwise quiet room. She sat up slowly, each vertebra connecting to the last in a wave. Katie drew a deep breath, centering herself, before she looked to her right at Jason's side of the room. For a moment, there was nothing. Katie let out the breath she was holding. Then the curtains fluttered.

Katie launched out of bed and across the room on a cloud of fear and adrenaline. The cool breeze from outside tickled the hairs on her arms as she stepped up to the window and looked out into the night. A dim light on the ground below her grabbed her attention. She blinked, brain trying to make sense of what she was seeing. The light had the form of a woman and shimmered white against the dark grass below it. As Katie watched, the woman looked up at her. Katie's skin seemed to burn even as she shivered bodily, unable to move or look away from the figure outside the window. The shining woman opened her mouth wide, as though she would scream. The screaming surrounded Katie like it was in the room and inside her head all at once.

Powerful hands shook her, gripping her shoulders. Katie could hear a deep voice shouting over the screaming that wouldn't stop. She recognized the voice as Jason's. He was shouting her name over and over, and with a shock, Katie realized she was the one screaming. Upon the realization, she stopped screaming and felt the burn in her throat that said she'd screamed much too hard for much too long and would be hoarse. Jason's shoulders sagged and his hands slacked on her shoulders. He pulled her to him, squeezing her tightly against his chest.

"You scared the shit out of me." His voice was gruff, still carrying a thread of fear. He moved Katie back to arms reach again, thumbs wiping away tears on her cheeks she hadn't even realized were there.

"You wanna tell me what that was about?"

"There was a woman outside the window." Jason turned his head toward it, and Katie followed his gaze. A cool tingle washed over her and bile climbed its way up her throat as she looked at the closed and latched window. "Did you close it?"

"No." Jason drew out the word so it was much longer than the one syllable should have been. His voice was low and careful, and Katie realized he was watching her like an animal that had been cornered and was ready to bolt.

"It was open." Katie's voice was rising in pitch, teetering on the edge of hysterics. "I heard the latch click, and then it was open when I walked over here. And I saw a woman."

"Katie, the window is closed, and there's no one out there. Do you think maybe you had a nightmare?" Jason's voice was calm and composed despite the crease between his eyebrows growing deeper with worry.

Katie traded her fear for anger. The heat of it starting deep in her stomach like a flickering candle ready to set the curtains alight. She was ready to rain that anger down on Jason for his audacity to question what she saw. Katie knew, in the back of her mind, that she was only this angry because she was also questioning herself. The word "crazy" kept reverberating around the space Liz used to occupy. She didn't care if her anger was misplaced and would have started the fight had a knock not come on the door just as she drew herself to her full five foot four.

Jason crossed to the door, and Katie deflated, struggling to rearrange her face in a pleasant manner. It only partly surprised her to see Darla outside the door, a long, green robe tied tight around her waist. Jason took a step back, opening the door wider, and motioned to invite Darla into the room.

"Sorry to intrude so late. But my room is three away, and I heard screaming." Darla looked from Jason to Katie expectantly.

"That was my fault. I'm so sorry I woke you." Katie sighed. Her gaze lingered on the closed window, and she quickly ran the possibilities through her head before turning back to look at Jason. "I guess I had a nightmare. It just felt so real." The flicker of anger inside her gave one last hot pulse before extinguishing.

"What was the nightmare about?" Darla asked, settling her bottom against the edge of the desk.

Jason looked at her, eyebrows halfway up his forehead, ready to be offended on Katie's behalf. She understood the reaction and knew that Darla's nosiness should probably offend her. But Katie was too tired to be offended, and she had the strangest sense that Darla's curiosity was well intentioned. There was something in the young woman's earnest face that made her feel understood. And feeling understood by a relative stranger felt better than questioning her own sanity.

"We went to bed with the window closed. I heard a creak in the floor, and then I heard the latch click. When I got up and crossed to the window, it was open." Katie stared at the window in question, daring it to open again right there in front of them. "When I went to close the window, I saw a woman. But she wasn't just a woman. It was like she was made of light."

"You saw The White Lady!" Darla exclaimed, crossing to the window and surveying the dark grounds.

"I'm sorry, the what?"

"The White Lady. She's one of the many ghosts here and the most active. Students see her all the time. The girls in the room below this always complain about footsteps even when this room is empty." Darla's voice was matter-of-fact, eyes still tracing the grounds.

"Oh, come on." Jason huffed a laugh. "Those are just stories older kids tell the incoming freshmen to spook them."

"Are they?" Darla asked mildly, one eyebrow raised.

"Katie?" Jason asked, hands spread, asking for

help.

"I know what I saw, Jason."

"And what did you see, Katelyn?"

"The White Lady."

Katie looked into Darla's eyes and knew that what she saw was real, that she wasn't crazy. There were things in the world that just couldn't be explained by the logic Jason was looking for. Or maybe Darla was just as crazy as she was.

THIRTEEN

KATIE LAZED ON A COUCH in the dorm rec room, slouched so far down that her chin touched her chest. She had a cup of coffee nestled against her sternum and a journal filled with messy scrawling open beside her. She scrolled intently through her phone. She'd been on the couch since she'd given up on sleep at three in the morning. Since then, she'd been neck-deep in research about Tranquil Heights' haunted history.

She'd found an episode of a ghost hunting TV show that had only lasted one season, many websites from amateur ghost hunters, and even a few blog posts from academics explaining why people probably thought they saw ghosts. She's learned that they thought the biggest culprit for ghost sightings was mold. The spores were already known to cause depression, anxiety, and delirium, among other mental effects. Why not add in hallucinations?

Though Katie had only been at Tranquil Heights for two nights and didn't think mold spores could have caused quite such a vivid hallucination so quickly, she had begun to second-guess what she had seen. She fought against that logic because the existence and possible connection to spirits on the Earth had given Katie a new hope.

Katie's phone buzzed in her hands. A photo of Jason and his message covered the information she was reading. *You okay?* Katie half smiled, glad to have married a person who cared so very much for her. *I'm okay. In the rec room.* Katie wasn't sure that "I'm okay" was the truth, but looking at the information on her phone, she thought that soon it would be.

Jason plopped down on the couch beside her, book bag slung over his shoulder. He threw an arm over her shoulders and kissed her three times in quick succession. They always kissed in quick groups of three as a hello or goodbye. One just never seemed like enough.

"What's on the curse breaking agenda today?" he asked.

"I'm actually going to an occult shop in Seattle to do some more research."

"Do they specialize in curses?"

"Something like that."

"Do you need me to go with you? I wouldn't ask, but I have a client who is having a marketing emergency and it's probably better if I handle it myself."

"No, I'm fine. You make that client happy, win that bread."

"In that case, I will be holed up in a corner of the dining room all day." Jason gave her a winning smile and planted three more kisses on her lips. "Have a good day. I'll see you when you get back. I love you."

Katie watched his broad shoulders as he walked away, glad that he would have something to keep him busy. She hadn't lied. She was going to an occult shop in Seattle. But it had nothing to do with breaking the curse. At least not directly.

Katie had realized last night that she was in far over her head at Tranquil Heights. She wasn't the one who adventured or braved the terrifying. Liz had always led the charge: fearless, assertive, and ready to take on the world. Katie had simply followed her sister, ready to support her how ever she needed, happy to offer kind words and hugs when things didn't go the way Liz had planned. She had no hope of forging a path forward and breaking this curse without Liz to hold the torch in the dark.

. . .

The Other Side Occult Shop specialized in the dead. Their website touted expertise in all things spirit realm: how to communicate with the dead, how to protect yourself from hauntings, and rituals to seal yourself if you were sensitive. The cloying scent of lavender incense hugged Katie as she walked into the shop. A light tinkle came from the bells hung from the doorknob, disrupting the otherwise eerie silence of the tiny space.

An older woman, wrapped in many layers of shawls and skirts, appeared from behind a stack of leather books. Stripes of gray streaked her thick, dark hair split into two French braids that lay over her shoulders to her waist.

"Welcome in. I'm Augustina." The woman reached out a pale, bony hand that appeareed almost translucent out to Katie.

"Hi. I'm Katie."

The woman held onto Katie's hand for longer than was polite. She tried to pull away, but Augustina's hand gripped hers tighter. The frailty was in looks only; the older woman was strong, and Katie stopped trying to pull away.

"The dead have touched you. It's all over you."

Augustina moved in closer to Katie, placing her face next to the younger woman's and inhaling deeply. "You smell of anger, fear, and heartbreak. Not all of it yours."

Katie pulled out of Augustina's grip and took a full step back. The pulse in her neck jumped and she taste pennies at the back of her throat. She rubbed her hand on her jeans as though the fear had been physically placed in it and she could simply wipe it away.

"I didn't mean to scare you. Please accept my apologies." Augustina raised her hands to appear nonthreatening.

"It's okay. I've been jumpy lately. It's not really your fault." Katie consciously took her hand away from her thigh, took a deep breath, and willed her heart rate to slow.

"I trust I'm correct about your recent encounters with the dead?" Augustina asked, making intense eye contact that made Katie uncomfortable. She simply nodded in response.

"You're here for protection then," the older woman stated before setting off for a shelf filled with various herbs.

"Actually, I'm here because I want to contact the dead." Katie followed at Augustina's heels, gripping the straps of her purse so hard she could feel her fingernails digging into her palms.

"I terrified you just by telling you the dead had touched you. Why would you want to contact them?"

"Not them. Just her."

"Who?"

"My sister."

"When did she pass?"

"Three weeks ago."

"You were close?"

"Closer than close. We're twins."

"I have to tell you, contacting the dead is a chaotic magic. The dead won't always respond in the ways you had thought or hoped they would."

"What does that mean?"

"You can't control the conversation. You can't even guarantee you'll find the right person to converse with. Delving into the spirit plane is part chaos and part genuine belief that you'll get what you need. It is not something you can, or should, do light-heartedly and without clear intentions." Augustina collected herbs and books as she spoke, moving easily between the tight tables and bookshelves. She turned to survey Katie with a furrowed brow, the slightest frown bringing out more wrinkles in her wizened face. "The dead are still themselves, but with fewer consequences."

Katie had read about the unpredictable nature of séances during the morning's furious Googling session, but it was different to hear it laid out so plainly by the mysterious Augustina. The older woman regarded her with a facial expression that married curiosity and infinite patience. Katie's thoughts ricocheted around her mind rapidly. Part of her wanted to flee, run screaming from the building with the last of her skepticism and sanity intact. The other part, the part questioning everything she thought she knew, wanted—needed—to find out if it was true. She had to try to contact Liz. She couldn't face the possibility of this curse being real without Liz.

"I have to try," Katie said. She searched Augustina's face for some hint that would tell her if she'd made the right decision, but the old woman's face was pleasantly passive. Katie took a deep breath and nodded, steeling her resolve. Augustina moved through the small shop and handed Katie everything she'd need with an explanation of the importance of each piece.

"The spirit realm isn't at all like our own, Katie. They don't have to play by the same rules. And spirits who are stuck on our plane are rarely polite. You must prepare for anything," Augustina said as she handed the bag over to Katie. She held onto the bag even as Katie's hand wrapped around its handle and searched the younger woman's face. Katie had the feeling that the older woman could see everything inside her. She wanted nothing more than to leave and never come back to this shop. "Gods be with you, Katie." Augustina's voice mixed with the tinkling of the bells on the door, creating an eerie melody that Katie wouldn't soon forget.

By the time Katie slipped into the car and placed the bag with candles, herbs, and a Ouija board in the passenger seat, it was past five in the evening and she'd arrive back at Tranquil Heights in time for dinner. She spent the entire drive repeating Augustina's instructions to herself, hoping she was prepared to do what she needed to come nightfall.

FOURTEEN

WHEN WILHELMINA WALKED into Tranquil Heights, it was silent, the kind of silence that weighed heavily on the shoulders of all those exposed to it. Wilhelmina knew that heavy silence. Something terrible had happened.

She crossed quickly to Violet whose solemn expression was so out of place on her youthful face, cursing her squeaky shoes.

"What is it? What's happened?" she asked, dread welling up in her stomach.

"It's Beatrice. They think she's miscarried."

Wilhelmina walked down the corridor of medical rooms in a daze. Beatrice was nearly six months pregnant. A miscarriage this late was shocking, horrifying, and so difficult for Wilhelmina to imagine as a mother. Here, in the long white corridor, the silence was gone. She could hear Dr. Covington asking for instruments and the clinking of trays and instruments as they passed from nurses to the doctor. Wilhelmina stood outside the door, watching with weary eyes, trying to summon the courage to step in and help—to do her job.

The scene in the patient room was overwhelming. The rooms were always white and gleaming, but with the addition of the medical lights, everything was almost heavenly bright. That is where the comparison to heaven ended, though. This was most certainly hell.

Wilhelmina knew how much blood the human body held but knowing it in theory and seeing blood soaking the white tile floor were two different things. So much blood—splatter across the white sheets, the white of Dr. Covington's coat, the white of the day nurse's uniform. Wilhelmina knew from looking at the red puddles and speckles there was no "thinking" Beatrice had miscarried. There was only knowing.

Wilhelmina watched as the orderlies gathered up blood-soaked rags. They, too, had started life as white cloth, but were now soaked so thoroughly with blood they looked black. They filled black bags with the rags, the sheets from the bed, the patient gown Beatrice was wearing. Wilhelmina stepped forward, taking a clean washcloth from atop an impossibly high stack. She laid it in a bowl of clean, warm water that the orderlies would change out frequently. She stationed herself next to Beatrice who had yet to look at her. Wilhelmina rubbed the cloth down Beatrice's blood-streaked legs,. The water ran down in streams of pink and soaked into the towels the orderlies had placed under her.

The deafening silence squeezed in around Wilhelmina and Beatrice as the other nurse and orderlies exited the room, each following tasks and protocols set in place for this situation. Wilhelmina and Beatrice sat alone in the silence. The color slowly returned to the young woman's skin. When she was clean and a stranger could no longer tell she'd been through a great tragedy, Wilhelmina dressed her in a fluffy white robe and escorted her back to her own room.

Wilhelmina was unsurprised Natalie and Alice waiting in Beatrice's room when they entered. She stepped back and allowed the women who had become Beatrice's friends to encircle her in their arms. Alice had pulled Beatrice's favorite comfort clothing out on the bed. Wilhelmina watched as the two women worked to dress their compatriot. She realized, with a shock, that though the silence had continued, it was no longer heavy or oppressive. There was something companionable in the air, a lightness she couldn't explain.

A knock came at the door, and Natalie, Beatrice, and Alice turned in tandem to stare at the it. There was something almost hopeful on their faces that Wilhelmina couldn't understand. She kept her eye on them as she crossed to the door and opened it. Violet stood outside the door, eyes wide, a faint tremor running through her entire body.

"Mr. Hatfield is here," she whispered. "He's here to see Beatrice. Not Connor, but his father."

"Beatrice, dear? Do you feel up to taking a visitor? Apparently, Mr. Hatfield is here to see you." Wilhelmina kept the door only partially opened as she asked, fully prepared to tell Violet to send him packing.

"I'll see him." Beatrice's voice was strong, sure. Wilhelmina's eyebrows raised, but she quickly gained control of her facial expression. Beatrice preened her clothing with the help of Natalie and Alice. Watching the three of them, Wilhelmina could have sworn that they'd been expecting him.

Wilhelmina opened the door wide and told Violet to bring Mr. Hatfield up. Patient rooms could be used for private meetings with visitors, but it was policy that a nurse or orderly be in the room to ensure the patient's safety. Wilhelmina waited at the still open door and watched Beatrice fidget impatiently. Mr.

Hatfield was a large man, standing two heads taller than Wilhelmina, putting him over six feet tall. In his youth, he had been broad and muscular, but as he'd aged that broadness had made way for a rotundness that only made him seem more imposing. His eyes were small in his round face, and they glanced over at Wilhelmina and Natalie, lingering on Alice before settling on Beatrice.

"Beatrice. Dr. Covington called. I came right away. It is my understanding that you no longer need to be here at Tranquil Heights?" He made it a question. He was a good businessman, and it was always best to confirm the facts rather than assume the truth.

"That's right. You and Connor no longer need to be worried about me." Beatrice kept her voice even, no inflections to hint at her mental state or feelings on the matter.

"Yes, well, there's still the matter of privacy."

"I'll keep your secrets. I know how this works. I'm ruined if I don't keep the secrets, so it's in my best interest to shut up."

A mottled flush crept up Mr. Hatfield's neck and face. Wilhelmina suppressed a chuckle. Beatrice was far from the gentility to which Mr. Hatfield was accustomed. She had a certain knack for telling it like it was, and it didn't matter who you were or where you were from.

"Yes, well, be that as it may." Mr. Hatfield cleared his throat and reached into his interior coat pocket. He withdrew a large envelope, tapping the end in his other hand. "I've purchased you a train ticket. My son told me you had dreams of California, so that's where you're going. You'll find enough money in the envelope to get you situated comfortably there."

He placed the envelope in Beatrice's outstretched hands. He looked at her for a long moment while she stared at the envelope. She finally nodded, and he seemed to find that confirmation enough. He cleared his throat again, gave a curt nod to both Natalie and Wilhelmina, and turned to walk out the door.

"Lovely to see you, Alice, as always." And with that, Mr. Hatfield was gone.

Alice flushed a beautiful shade of pink and smiled broadly at Natalie and Beatrice, whose wide grins matched hers. The air in the room seemed to crackle with excitement, and Wilhelmina thought she smelled something fresh and clean, like the moment after it rains.

· · ·

Beatrice appeared in the grand entryway to the

patient building the next afternoon, large suitcase in one hand, envelope from Mr. Hatfield clutched tightly in the other. She'd spent the morning saying her goodbyes to various patients and packing her entire life into the one suitcase. Her face appeared younger and shined with the excitement of dreams coming true.

Wilhelmina waited by the door, ready to see her into the taxi waiting to take her to the train station. Natalie and Alice stood next to her, emanating a mixture of sadness of losing their friend and happiness that she was getting what she wanted.

"Hang in there. You'll be okay," Beatrice said as she hugged Alice tightly to her. "You deserve the world. Never forget that."

"Thank you for everything." Beatrice threw her arms around Natalie. "I never would have realized how much I could do without you. You've changed my whole life."

Natalie and Alice stood beaming, arms linked as they watched Beatrice settle herself into the taxi. They waved until the car had bumped far enough down the lane, past the trees.

Wilhelmina found a peaceful smile spreading across her face as she realized how such a terrible situation had turned itself into a positive one. She met Natalie's knowing eyes as she climbed back up the stairs into the building.

"Life has a way of balancing itself out," Natalie said before grabbing Alice's hand and leaving Wilhelmina to wonder for the second time what exactly that meant.

FIFTEEN

"KATIE, COULD YOU JUST SLOW DOWN and think about this with me for a minute?" Jason paced the floor in front of their bed, hands on his hips.

"I have already thought about this, Jason." Katie was laying out her supplies in careful patterns exactly as Augustina had told her. The large white candle was settled into a pile of salt on a saucer. To bind the spirit, Augustina had said. Little dishes contained herbs waiting for Katie to burn them: cedarwood, wormwood, and myrrh. The Ouija board lay in the middle of these little dishes, the candle placed to one side. On the other side, Katie placed a photo of Liz.

"Katie, please stop and look at me." Jason had stopped pacing, and Katie turned to look at him from her kneeling position. He kneeled on the carpet in front of her and grabbed her hands. "I am here to support you in whatever way you need. But that doesn't mean that I'm going to blindly let you do whatever you want. It's still my job to take care of you, to protect you, and that includes protecting you from yourself."

"I'm not crazy, Jason." She sighed and squeezed his hands. "I understand why you feel the way you do. I really do. But I need you to open your mind just a little bit and see this from my perspective. My sister died on her twenty-fifth birthday. She's the fourth firstborn daughter in my family to do that. You know I've never believed in my family's ridiculous curse. But here we are, three weeks after Liz's death. And I can't just assume it's a hysterical imagining turned self-fulfilling prophecy. All the deaths are too accidental for that."

"I don't disagree. It's a bit much to be a coincidence. Even I concede that."

"Yes. Exactly. And if the curse is real, maybe other things are real, too. This place has a long history of hauntings. Many people have seen things here. And I'm positive I wasn't dreaming last night, Jason."

"I see your point. And I believe that you believe you weren't sleeping. I'll suspend my disbelief and say you saw a ghost last night. But," Jason sighed and gestured at the things on the floor. "What do the ghosts and the contacting of the dead have to do with the curse? We're supposed to be here figuring out the origins of the curse, not talking to ghosts."

"Because if the paranormal is real, if all these things we've been telling ourselves aren't real, actually are... then I can talk to Liz. And I don't think I can break this curse without her."

Jason looked like Katie had slapped him across the face. He looked at the items on the floor, eyes lingering on the photo of Liz, before he let out a deep sigh. He placed his hands on either side of Katie's face and kissed her forehead. "I think you can do a lot more than you give yourself credit for, Katie. But if it's that important to you, I'm here. I'll put my hands on that little thing with the Ouija board. I'll help you try to talk to Liz. Just tell me what to do."

Katie's shoulders sagged with relief. She knew she couldn't do the big, hard things without Liz, but she was also pretty sure she couldn't do them without Jason. Some people become security blankets, and you need them to get through your day to day, let alone curse breakings and hauntings.

"Okay, you come sit next to me." Katie sat with her legs crossed in front of her, closer to Liz's photo. She patted the ground next to her and handed him a box of matches as he scooted in close. "Light the herbs first, then the candle."

Jason did as he was told, and the aroma from the herbs was both intense and soothing in a way that called to a primal part of Katie. She breathed the scent in deeply, centering herself, and letting a calmness take root deep inside her.

Katie placed her hands on the planchette and looked pointedly at Jason. He blew out a breath, rolled his shoulders, and placed his fingertips next to Katie's. They shared a moment, staring into each other's eyes—blue eyes filled with hope and belief, brown eyes squinting and outlined by the furrow of the brow. Katie nodded at Jason before tilting her head back, eyes closed.

"Are there any spirits here?" Augustina had explained that it was best to first establish if there were any spirits in the area that could interfere with calling to a distinct spirit. It was possible that the spirit in the area was the one being sought after, but it was always best to know definitively if something was there before calling the spirit in question.

The planchette moved under Katie's fingers and her head snapped down, eyes flying wide in shock. Though Katie had certainly wanted to believe— needed to believe—she hadn't given up her skepticism. She glanced at Jason, whose brows had raised, leaving deep wrinkles in his forehead. He shook his head almost imperceptibly, letting Katie know he was not moving the planchette to mess with her. She supposed it was possible that she was doing it subconsciously, but as the planchette crept its way across the board to cover the "yes" option, Katie didn't think that was true.

Jason inhaled sharply and she looked at him. He studied the word "yes" as though he'd never considered its meaning before. Katie let out a shaky breath, ready to ask another question, but before she could, the planchette moved again, much faster this time. Katie fought to keep her hands on the planchette. A deep ache rose in her shoulders as she denied the reflex to pull away. The muscles in Jason's arms twitch and his eyebrows knit together in concentration. He was fighting the same impulse to get away.

"B—A—B—Y," Katie spelled out, following the planchette. Her breath caught in her throat, and she felt that sharp pinching sensation at the corner of her eyes that meant tears were imminent. "Yes, Liz! I'm pregnant."

The planchette set off again. Jason had grown still beside her, and she spared a quick glance at him. His eyes were wide, lips parted, his chest rose and fell in quick jerks. Katie realized with a jolt that Jason was scared. She had stopped being scared and was only excited now, overjoyed to be contacting her sister.

"G—I—R—L," Katie spelled out again, head following the planchette as it moved from letter to letter. She lifted her head, looking around the room, half expecting to see Liz's face, eyes filled with mischievous humor. The room was just as empty as it had been, but Katie kept her head up as she spoke. "Yes, Liz. I was afraid of that. That's why we're here. I'm trying to figure out how the curse started. I need your help."

The room filled with a warmth that reminded Katie of those nights when she and Liz had snuggled together in Liz's bed, warding off the boogeyman. A brief flicker tugged at Katie's mind, and she could feel that place inside her that had always belonged to Liz fill up. The warmth continued to grow into a heat and the room crackled with an energy that made Katie's skin crawl. Flashes of heat bit into the skin on her arms, so hot they almost felt cold, like when the bacon grease pops out of the pan.

"Katie, I don't think this is Liz," Jason said. "It feels... angry."

When the heat came to a tipping point, a wind whipped through the room. The paper copy of the journal went flying, pages dancing in a circle around them. Katie realized the candle was still flickering, no sign of the wind impacting the flame. She and Jason were in the eye of a small cyclone in their room.

"Where is this coming from? The window isn't even open!" Jason's head whipped around as he tried to find the source of the wind. As if on cue, the window on Jason's side of the room flew open with a crash that shook the panes. He pulled his hands off the planchette and leaped to his feet. Fight or flight mode had taken over for him, and he was ready to face whatever foe came through the window.

Katie watched the window with wide eyes, fingers still on the planchette, and knew that there would be no physical being for Jason to lay hands on. There was no way for him to stop what was happening and protect them. A shining light appeared at the window, hazy through the dust, papers, and even clothing the cyclone had picked up.

Katie felt a heat well up inside of her. It was heavy and thick, and she was choking on it. She recognized the sensation as anger, but it was unlike anything she had ever felt. She opened her mouth to scream, and a long, ragged shriek of unadulterated rage fell from her lips. It felt for all the world like a gigantic snake uncoiled itself from depths of her body and wound its way lazily out of her mouth. When there seemed to be a hollow place where all that anger had been, Katie stopped screaming. She breathed heavily, still sitting on the floor, hands on the planchette.

Jason was looking from Katie to the shimmering presence that had not yet solidified. She stood up, nodding in reassurance at Jason. She was okay. They were okay.

She stepped up next to Jason and took his hand. Her own anger built inside her, a cool and calculating feeling to counteract all that emotional heat The White Lady brought on. She was angry because she was almost sure she had been talking to Liz before The White Lady came to interfere. She reached into herself and found Liz's place still full of a tickling warmth, like the wind coming off the Puget Sound in August.

The shimmering form sharpened, and The White Lady took shape in front of their eyes. It was difficult to make sense of what she looked like, as one part of her faded into another, blocked by the light that seemed to emanate from her. Katie thought she must have been blonde in life, because her hair shone brighter than other parts of her. It fell in stringy clumps around her face, as though she had been wet when she died. She wore a non-descript white hospital gown, which made it impossible for Katie to determine what era she may have been from. She could have been a TB patient from the earliest days of Tranquil Heights, or even a mental patient who died just before the facility closed its doors as a hospital.

"Oh my god," Jason whispered beside her. His jaw had gone slack, mouth hanging open. His eyes were wide, and he blinked slowly, processing what he was seeing at a snail's pace. Katie watched his chest rise and fall with deep, slow breaths. It was as if everything about him had slowed down.

Katie turned back to survey The White Lady. The figure was surveying her back, head tilted to one side. The wind died down and The White Lady took slow, deliberate steps towards Katie. The heat in the room dissipated, quickly replaced by a bone chilling cold. She likened it to standing in dense fog as she watched Jason's breath form clouds in front of his face. A fine tremor started in his body, echoed in her own.

"What do we do, Katie?" Jason asked between chattering teeth.

Katie cast her gaze around the room wildly, searching for anything that could help. She landed on the candle, still flickering atop its plate of salt. She shut her eyes tight, making little shapes burst in front of her eyes. She dug deep, thinking about her conversation with Augustina. Had that really only been earlier that afternoon? She felt as though time had both stood still and sped up. Certainly it had been many days since she had visited The Other Side, not just many hours. *A candle to bind the spirit. You don't want to be setting anything malevolent loose on accident. Salt to combat negative energies. You may wish to place a line of salt across the doors of your space.*

Katie cursed herself. She had been so eager to reach Liz, she hadn't thought to salt the doors. *Though it's chaos magic, and as such can be unpredictable, remember that you are still in charge. You start the ritual; you close it. The single most important thing you will do is to remember that it is your power, your control that opens and closes this curtain to the beyond.*

Katie opened her eyes, filled with the certainty that she knew what to do, and more than that, she *could* do it. She kneeled next to the board and flipped it over. No need to have a way to contact the dead when they were right in front of you, making everything cold and miserable. She poured salt water on the burning herbs, snuffing them out, and with them the power they called. Katie carefully picked up the plate with the salt and candle. She stood facing The White Lady and gathered every ounce of resolve she had.

"You are not welcome here. I did not call you." Katie blew out the candle and watched The White Lady. Nothing happened.

"I was here first, girl. No one calls me here but me." A voice slithered through the room, causing Katie and Jason to shudder. The voice was hushed and husky, as though it hadn't been used for a long time. The White Lady continued to take deliberate steps towards Katie and Jason, but her eyes were fixed on the corner of the room. The closer she got, the more it felt like Katie was being submerged in a freezing lake. She struggled to breathe past the cold. She wondered for a moment if this is what it felt like to drown.

The world narrowed down to just her and The White Lady. The ghost was within one step of Katie, and everything seemed to slow down. She watched her own hand reach for the salt on the plate with a detached sense that she was doing the right thing. The salt felt solid and grounding in her hand, and warmth seeped back into her fingers as she ground the edges of the grains into her hand. Just as The White Lady started to take that last step to close the gap between them, Katie threw the handful of salt directly at the ghost's face with a strangled scream that came out sounding like "No!"

The White Lady dissipated into a shimmering, formless fog again that floated backwards toward the still open window. The hushed voice filled the room, wrapping Katie in its angry heat, making her nerves misfire and ache after the extreme cold.

"You can't really be rid of me. The other ghosts and I... we are Tranquil Heights." The White Lady came back into focus again for just a moment, staring into the room with an expression close to disdain. Jason crossed to Katie and gripped her hand tightly. His stance told her he was ready to run from the room, pulling her with him.

"Tranquil Heights is us." The White Lady sighed before stepping backwards through the wall that held the window and disappearing into the night.

SIXTEEN

TRANQUIL HEIGHTS
FEBRUARY 1935

ALICE PULLMAN SAT AT A TABLE in the corner of the dining room by herself. She had a book open on the table in front of her, but she paid no attention to it. Her gaze was fixed on something outside the window, or maybe on nothing at all. It was raining, but the temperature hovered close to that space where rain becomes snow, and drops too thick to be rain were becoming more common.

Wilhelmina watched Alice watch the rapidly changing downpour, and a crease formed between the nurse's eyebrows. Normally Alice was a beacon of hope and light in Tranquil Heights. Despite her situation, there was something innocent and shiny about Alice, like she was brand new. She looked at everything through a positive lens and could be relied upon to help others make the best of their bad days. Being in the same room with Alice often brought a sense of warm contentment to Wilhelmina. It was as though she projected her easy happiness the same way Beatrice projected her anger. Today, Alice's light was dim. There was a sadness pouring from her that Wilhelmina had never seen before.

Wilhelmina sat in the chair across from Alice, hands atop the table, fingers interlaced. Alice turned her head for a fraction of a moment before returning to staring out the window. They sat that way in silence for five minutes, though to Wilhelmina it felt like much longer.

Finally, Alice sighed and turned her full attention to Wilhelmina. "Do you need something, Willy?"

Wilhelmina drew a deep breath. She hated when the patients called her Willy though usually she gave Alice a pass because it was accompanied with a brilliant smile and eyes shimmering with good will. The childlike quality to Alice's demeanor made everyone at Tranquil Heights just a little more lenient on her.

"I think it's more a matter of you needing something, Alice."

"And what is it you think I need?" Alice's tone was direct, harsh. Her normal tone was breathy and lilting, like she was always laughing at an inside joke no one else understood. The Alice in front of Wilhelmina was so grown up, so jaded, and it made Wilhelmina's heart ache.

"Someone to talk to, I'd wager. You've been staring out this window for most of the day. It's like someone's gone and snuffed your light."

"Maybe I'm just realizing what everyone else already knew about me."

"What's that?"

"That I've been naïve." Alice huffed a sad laugh. "So incredibly stupid."

"You aren't stupid, Alice."

"I thought he loved me, Willy." Alice's eyes were wide and shiny as she looked at Wilhelmina. Tears threatened to spill over the edge, and Alice forced them still wider, he surface tension holding the liquid in place.

"That isn't stupid, Alice. It's human. He told you he loved you. Why wouldn't you have believed him?"

"I thought when I told him I was pregnant, we'd get married. I never once thought I'd end up here with another woman pregnant by him." Alice's tone was so bitter, it left a flavor on Wilhelmina's tongue almost like vomit. "Not to say that I'm angry with Beatrice. She had no idea about me, just as I had no idea about her. We have to stick together, us women wronged by Connor Hatfield."

"See, you're not stupid. You know not to be angry

at Beatrice when you should be angry at Connor." Wilhelmina watched as a tear broke free and slid down Alice's face. The young woman wiped at it quickly, and her lips curved upwards by the tiniest degree.

"She writes me, you know? From California. She's found a job she enjoys in a club there. How anyone could have found a job that fast in these times." Alice shook her head.

"She's clearly got someone or something looking out for her," Wilhelmina agreed.

"She does. Only it's not what you think. The someone or something looking out for Beatrice is Beatrice. She has this way of just setting her mind to something and doing it."

"You're probably right."

"I wish I was more like Beatrice."

"So you could set your mind to it and just do it?"

"Yes. I just don't seem to have strong enough thoughts."

"Well... what are you setting your mind to?"

Alice was quiet for several minutes as she regarded Wilhelmina carefully. Tears spilled over her eyelids and slid in tracks down her cheeks to form quivering drops at her jawline, waiting to release. She took a deep breath and looked back out the window.

"This is where I tell you again that I am stupid, Willy." Alice raised her hand. She was still looking out the window but seemed to know that Wilhelmina was preparing to argue. "What I want, still, is to marry Connor Hatfield. To raise this child in a comfortable home, never wanting for anything." She turned to face Wilhelmina again jaw tense. There was a darkness to her hazel eyes that dared Wilhelmina to shame her, to confirm that she was stupid.

"That's a smart thing to want." Wilhelmina smiled as Alice lifted one eyebrow, searching for the explanation. "You want a father for your baby. Anyone would. And the biological father of your baby is rich. Of course you'd want that man to marry you and take care of you and yours. It's perfectly logical."

"I suppose you're right. It's not what Beatrice wanted though, is it?"

"Beatrice didn't want the baby at all. You do."

"I do." Alice wrapped her arms around her enormous belly. She only had a month to go, and every day seemed to be larger than the last. "But not alone. Not like this. I want to be married and to raise my baby without struggle."

"Oh, Alice." Wilhelmina sighed. "I know. I don't blame you. I'd want the same thing. We just don't always get what we want."

"Beatrice did."

"That she did. But Beatrice's wants only involved her. No one else needed to make life-altering decisions for her to get what she wanted."

"So this is it? I must struggle to raise this baby

alone, and Connor gets to continue living his perfect cushioned life? I lose my reputation. I harm my family's reputation. And the Hatfields get out without a scratch." Alice's voice rose with every declaration. She smashed her palm down on the table in front of her. "It's not fair, Willy."

"It's not."

"I won't."

"You won't?"

"I absolutely refuse to lose everything and do this by myself." Alice struggled to her feet from the chair. "I will not be this woman."

Wilhelmina watched Alice move through the dining room, eyebrows raised. Goosebumps had broken out on her arms, and she wasn't sure why, but she believed Alice. Wilhelmina didn't think Alice could do anything about her situation. She'd been at Tranquil Heights for four months already and the Hatfields hadn't bothered to visit once. Connor Hatfield would not marry Alice, Wilhelmina knew, but she also inexplicably knew that Alice would not leave here without a father for her baby.

Wilhelmina turned as she stood up and found herself looking directly at Natalie, who was watching her with narrowed eyes, head tilted to one side. Wilhelmina began to wipe her palms on her thighs, stopped herself, and turned on her heel to exit the dining room. She felt a prickle at the base of her spine that let her know Natalie was still watching her. She had to force herself to keep a moderate pace rather than running from that strange sensation.

SEVENTEEN

SOMETHING HAD WOKEN DARLA late at night, an energy she had never felt in all her years at Tranquil Heights. The air was heavy the way it was after a summer rain. Goosebumps broke out across her body, the tiny hairs vibrating with some primal knowledge that not all was well. She walked down the hall to room 302, fighting the urge to turn around and run with every step.

She made it to the door and pushed it open just as a shimmering light faded through the wall. The air was immediately cooler and easier to breathe, and Darla took in the state of the Edgecombs' room in shock. There were papers strewn about the floor, lamps knocked over, and in the middle of the open space in front of the desk stood Katie Edgecomb, saucer of salt in hand. The air seemed to crackle around her, and Darla felt a shift, as though the Katie Edgecomb who had come here just days ago was not the Katie Edgecomb who stood in the center of the room.

Katie calmly set the saucer she was holding on the floor and pulled Jason towards the door. She came to an abrupt stop as she noticed Darla standing there. Katie's face hardened, a deep knowledge and understanding filling her eyes. She brushed past, forcing Darla to take a step back or be knocked aside.

"Darla, we would like a new room. Now. We'll be in the rec room waiting for you."

Darla raised her eyebrows as Katie and Jason disappeared through the door at the end of the hallway. A fresh wave of goosebumps broke out over her body and a trickle of sweat slid down her back as she looked back into the room at the drowned herbs, the candle, the upside-down Ouija board.

Darla quickly got Katie and Jason situated in room 305, the one directly next to hers. She laid awake the rest of the night, wondering what exactly had happened in room 302 that had changed Katie Edgecomb from a sweet, frightened lamb to a lioness in charge.

.   .   .

Darla stood in the museum, third cup of coffee in hand. It was open house day at Tranquil Heights, a time each spring when parents would bring their beloved teenage girls to tour the facilities and decide if this prep school were the right answer for their precious brilliant angels. She remembered her tour day. She'd been sullen on the drive here, angry at the idea of being sent off to a boarding school away from the friends with which she'd grown up. But as soon as they'd crested the top of the driveway and saw Tranquil Heights in all her glory, she'd know that this was the place for her. It seemed to call to her, beckoning her to learn all its stories and its mysteries.

She'd fallen in love that spring day, and she'd chosen to stay when the opportunity presented itself. Darla was sure that when it came time for her to graduate and move on that Tranquil Heights was just as sad to see her go as she was to leave. The museum manager had quit the day before graduation, something about being tired of things never being where she left them and the perpetual feeling of being watched had sent her packing. Darla thought that was Tranquil Heights' clever way of making a space for her to stay, and she'd jumped at the chance.

Turning her attention to the present, she watched as girls and their parents excitedly walked the grounds deep in discussion about the curriculum, the extracurriculars, and the success rate of the students who went on to college. She watched curiously as one girl broke off from the rest of the tour group and took a seat on one bench in the courtyard. The girl seemed to stare at something in the gazebo, though as far as Darla could see, it was empty. Darla walked outside and stood next to the bench, looking down at the girl, who was still fixated on the gazebo.

"Hi, I'm Darla," she said as she took a seat on the bench next to the girl. She jumped and turned to look at Darla, blue eyes wide.

"I'm Paige." Darla noted Paige's rigid posture. The girl's eyes flickered toward the gazebo, and Darla could tell it took a lot of self control to bring them back to meet hers.

"Are you not enjoying your tour, Paige?"

"Oh, um..." Paige took a long pause and once again looked at the gazebo. "It's not that the tour is bad. This seems like a great school. I mean, it's beautiful..." She trailed off, a flush creeping up her cheeks.

"But?" Darla nudged Paige with her shoulder. "It's okay if you don't love it. It's not for everyone."

"It's just... it's different here."

"Different how?"

"There's so much..." Paige's hands made little circles in the air in front of her, searching for a word. "History. There's just a lot of history here."

"That's true. The grounds are old, and this place wasn't always a comfortable, top-end school."

"No, it wasn't." Paige's voice carried a rare

bitterness for someone so young. Her shoulders sagged under the weight of old knowledge.

"It isn't just history here for you, is it, Paige?"

Paige's head snapped away from the gazebo, gaze settling on Darla with a wary anticipation. "I've been here for six years. I started as a student here. Now I'm a history student at U Dub, and I run the museum here. I know almost everything there is to know about Tranquil Heights... including the inhabitants who never left."

Paige's eyes widened, her breathing picking up in pace. She switched her focus between the gazebo and Darla, weighing her choices. She finally settled on Darla's face, an eagerness glowing out of the young girl's eyes. "You can see them, too?"

"I can see some of them. But only sometimes." Paige's shoulders dropped, and the eagerness in her eyes was replaced with a sad loneliness that Darla wished to chase away. "I can feel them, though. It's like they've been whispering to me since I first got here, clamoring to tell me theirs stories." Darla nodded at the gazebo. "That one there, in the gazebo. Do you see a man?"

"Yes, in a hospital gown. He has bruises on his neck and his face is all purple."

"His name was Peter Gibbons. He was a patient here. They found him hanging from the rafters of that gazebo in 1954. He's why the rafters aren't exposed anymore."

"He's the fifth one I've seen since we got here fifteen minutes ago. And I think more are just at the edges of my vision. Almost like they are walking with me but staying just outside of peripherals." Paige sighed heavily. "I've seen them since I was little. But this place... there's so much pain here. It's so angry and filled with death."

"You aren't wrong. There is anger here. And it is filled with death. But it's not all angry."

"No, some of it's sad. But I think, with the dead, sadness is just a type of anger."

Darla sat in silence with Paige, thinking about how to respond and how to show the girl the beauty at Tranquil Heights. She grabbed Paige's hand and pulled her to her feet, guiding her to the museum. Darla thought if she could see the history, not just the ghosts, maybe Paige would feel better about the place.

As they walked through the door, a prickling sensation ran a track from the base of Darla's skull down her spine. She shuddered heavily, and Paige ripped her hand away, rubbing it as though the sensation had traveled from Darla to her.

The lights dimmed, then increased in brightness until Darla and Paige had to hold their hands up in front of their eyes. The faint buzzing fluorescent lights always gave off grew louder, a colony of angry bees on the defensive. There were popping noises followed by the sound of breaking glass, and the room darkened all at once. The only light left in the museum streamed in from the floor-to-ceiling windows on one side. Darla could hear nothing but the whooshing of her heartbeat in her ears and Paige's heavy breathing beside her.

At first, everything was quiet. There was no movement, no whisper of heating and cooling system, no life. Then a gentle breeze flitted about the room, playing with Darla's curls and ruffling Paige's pixie cut. A sheet of paper lifted off the entry desk to the museum and floated lazily along the current of wind before settling gently to the floor. Darla stepped forward to pick up the paper, Paige at her heels. Darla recognized the paper as a copy of the last page of Wilhelmina's journal. She'd been re-reading the book, Katie Edgecomb's presence bolstering her curiosity. The breeze picked up to a full wind, becoming the violent winds one might expect on the coast, but not inside a closed building.

The pages of Wilhelmina's original journal flipped, the old and fragile paper making a stiff, crinkling noise with each page turn. The pages flipped faster, and Darla's breathing matched the pace. The journal lived in an airtight, temperature-controlled box to preserve it from further moisture damage. There was no way for the wind to be in that box. There was no way for wind to be in the museum at all.

Darla glanced at Paige, and the girl had gone pale

and gray. Her eyes flicked from the journal and up, a furrow appearing between her brows. "She wants you to see something."

"Who wants me to see something? Is she talking to you?"

"I don't know her name. She's not speaking. Some of them talk to me and some of them don't. I can feel that she's angry, that she wants someone to understand something. Maybe about her? Or about her life? I get flashes of feeling, but I can't always be sure what they want."

"What does she look like?"

"She's dressed in a hospital gown. She's very pale and her skull is caved in on one side. It's like all the color's been washed out of her, except the blood. I've never seen one look like this."

"The White Lady."

"I'm sorry, what?"

"It's what the students have named her. She's the only one anyone has ever laid eyes on... at least that I know of, until you. She has appeared to a handful of students over time, but she's not detailed. She just shows up as a white figure."

As they watched, the pages of the journal stopped flipping, and the book lay open and still at the end, where there was evidence of several pages being ripped out of the book. Darla walked up to the case and stared down at the journal.

"I don't understand. What does she want me to see?"

"I think she's mad about the missing pages. I think there's information in them she wants you to have."

"I wish I could have that information, too. The pages were gone when we found the journal. The contractors searched high and low for them when they were remodeling. No one ever found them."

The journal in the case slammed shut and a rumble so low they could hardly hear it replaced the silence. The ground shook under Darla and Paige's feet. Darla grabbed Paige's hand and pulled her under the entry desk. In all her time at Tranquil Heights, Darla had never experienced an earthquake. She was about to say as much to Paige when a moaning started somewhere beyond the desk. The moan grew in pitch and volume until it was a shattering scream that made Darla's veins run with ice. The quaking had stopped, replaced once again with the violent wind. Papers whipped around the room, and Paige bounded out from under the desk and back into the courtyard before Darla could extract herself from the desk.

Darla watched through the large picture windows as Paige grabbed each of her parents by a hand and dragged them back towards the parking lot. Darla couldn't hear what Paige was saying, but she could see by the confused expressions on her parents' faces that it was likely the truth. She had a feeling she would not be seeing Paige back here come fall term, and she hoped the found a calmer school with fewer ghosts.

Darla turned back to the room, taking in the mess of papers on the floor and the journal in its case once again open to the first page as it usually was. She did not know what Katie Edgecomb had done the night before, but whatever it was, it seemed to have woken up the long sleeping ghosts of Tranquil Heights.

EIGHTEEN

WILHELMINA SAT IN A CORNER of the common room, crocheting a pale-yellow sweater for her daughter to wear at Easter. She looked up every few stitches, ensuring that the calm atmosphere of the room stayed that way. While she enjoyed her husband's reactions to the stories of cat fights and dramatic attempted breakouts, she cherished these calm days at Tranquil Heights. The patients watched television, read books, or partnered off to play games, and Wilhelmina and the orderlies could bring down their own tension levels in response.

A shadow fell across the yarn in Wilhelmina's hands, and she looked up to find Natalie standing over her. Natalie chewed on her bottom lip, hands holding on to each other. And it occurred to Wilhelmina that this was the first time she'd seen the young woman show anything short of utmost confidence. Wilhelmina carefully stashed her work in the basket on the floor next to her and gestured for Natalie to sit in the chair next to hers. Natalie took the seat, angling herself towards Wilhelmina awkwardly because of her growing belly.

"Can I do something for you, Natalie?" Wilhelmina's voice was careful and controlled. While she had written off the events of Christmas Eve as her own over-reaction, she would admit only to herself that Natalie's arrogant and abruptly honest nature made her uncomfortable.

"I was just wondering if you know what the plans are for my baby."

"I'm not sure what you mean."

"Yes you do. I'm here because Mr. Cumberland doesn't want a bastard infant born out of infidelity to ruin his chances at Governor. Josiah Cumberland has plans for everything. So, what exactly does he have planned for me and my baby?"

Wilhelmina locked eyes with Natalie, weighing her options. She was certain that Natalie could handle the truth. The woman was powerful, smart, and independent. Whatever Wilhelmina told her, she wouldn't fall to pieces and become a wreck for the next several weeks. Still, she had concerns that the news would spur Natalie into action that Wilhelmina would want no part of. Wilhelmina sighed deeply and cursed herself as she came to her decision.

"The Cumberland baby is to be sent to an orphanage under the name of Baby Doe. There can be no tracing it back to Senator Cumberland, you know that."

"I figured as much." The wind whipped the branches of the leafless trees out the window. Natalie stared outside and rubbed her stomach in an absent-minded way that made Wilhelmina's heart ache. "I need your help, Wilhelmina." Natalie's voice was soft, strained. She had lost her arrogant edge, her eyes were becoming wild, and Wilhelmina felt panic fill her own stomach.

"What would you have of me, Natalie?"

"I want this baby."

"Natalie—"

"No, Wilhelmina, just listen for a moment." Natalie's eyes compelled Wilhelmina to give her a chance, and with an impatient sigh, she sat back in her chair and nodded. "By all accounts, I shouldn't want this baby. Mr. Cumberland isn't a man who is told no. We all cave to him eventually. And when we do, we're rewarded with bonuses, paid vacation days, a dinner out paid for by the great and wonderful Mr. Cumberland. Aren't we so lucky to work for such a kind and caring man?"

"Natalie, why didn't you tell us? We could have

helped much sooner. We can call the police."

"Come, Wilhelmina, you aren't so naïve as that."

Wilhelmina and Natalie sat in silence while Wilhelmina's thoughts raced. Natalie was, of course, right. It was naïve to believe that the police would take the word of a maid over the word of an influential rich man. Senator Cumberland was very popular with police leadership in the area, as he'd secured funding for them during a lengthy budgetary debate. Natalie would be put down as just making trouble, and Senator Cumberland's reputation would remain intact.

"Okay, you're right. But the same logic applies to you keeping the baby, Natalie. You said it yourself, Senator Cumberland won't risk the hit to his reputation."

"That's true," Natalie said with a duck of her head. "But I could go away. The Cumberlands could buy me a one-way ticket to anywhere. I'd go away and never speak to them again. No one has to know about me or this baby."

"The idea isn't without merit, but how do you expect me to help with it?"

"Just bring up the idea to Dr. Covington. I know he's sympathetic. I know he hates the idea of tearing babies away from mothers. I've heard him talk to the orderlies about it."

"Again, you are not wrong. But we need to have a

conversation about your propensity for sneaking around where you don't belong."

Natalie sat back in her chair with a graceful shrug. She had the good sense to look sheepish for a moment before her face split into a wide, glowing grin. Wilhelmina couldn't help but smile back. No matter what emotions Natalie was feeling, they rubbed off on those around her.

"I will talk to Dr. Covington, but that's all I can promise."

"That's all I asked for, Wilhelmina." Natalie pushed herself out of her chair nimbly for someone seven months pregnant. "Thank you, Wilhelmina. I just know you'll be able to convince Dr. Covington, and he'll be able to convince Mr. Cumberland."

"And if he can't?"

The smile fell away from Natalie's face, and darkness shifted through her clear blue eyes. Wilhelmina pulled her sweater tighter around her, though she wasn't sure if the room had actually chilled or she had because of Natalie's change in demeanor.

"Mr. Cumberland ruined my life, Wilhelmina. The only bright spot is this little life growing inside me. If I can't raise this baby, if I can't watch him or her grow up... I have nothing left to live for." Natalie turned on her heel and left the common room following her ominous declaration.

Wilhelmina shook her head as Natalie walked

away. A small voice in the back of her head whispered in worried tones that the young woman was putting her faith in the wrong places. It was unlikely that Senator Cumberland would allow Natalie to disappear with the baby, as she suggested. Wilhelmina didn't believe appealing to his better nature would work since Natalie had just revealed that he didn't seem to have a better nature. But Wilhelmina knew, as she thought of the love she had for her own little girl, that she would do everything she could to help Natalie keep her own baby.

NINETEEN

WILHELMINA, VIOLET, AND JUSTIN pretended to be busy, risking surreptitious glances at Mr. and Mrs. Hatfield and their son Connor as they filed past the first floor nurse's station. Alice had given birth to a perfect baby boy that morning, and Dr. Covington had announced to a shocked staff that the Hatfields would come to visit Alice and the baby. Though Wilhelmina often chided Violet and Justin for gossiping, she was not immune to the intrigue the Hatfields' visit caused on the ward. It was for this reason that she was pleased when Dr. Covington called her in to speak with her shortly after the Hatfields arrived.

Wilhelmina would typically take a seat in one of the chairs opposite Dr. Covington's desk, but she stopped short upon entry to his office. Mr. and Mrs.

Hatfield occupied the two chairs, and Connor leaned up against the wall behind them, resolutely looking at anything but the people in the room. He was handsome, over six feet tall like his father, the same physical prowess clear under his custom-tailored suit. The room smelled of roses and cedar, a tantalizing mixture of Mrs. Hatfield's perfume and the mens' aftershave, subtle in the way that only really expensive fragrances are.

"Nurse Darrington, I need you to help Alice pack her things. She will be going home with the Hatfields."

Wilhelmina struggled to maintain an expression of neutral pleasantness as a thrill of shock worked its way up her spine and settled as a tingling sensation on her scalp. Before she could ask questions, Mrs. Hatfield spoke up.

"We've discussed this at length, and at twenty two, it's time for Connor to get serious about his life. He'll be taking up a position in Vernon's company, and it naturally follows that he should take a wife and settle down." Mrs. Hatfield gazed at Wilhelmina in earnest, large eyes pleading with her to understand.

"The Pullmans are an excellent family. Prominent, respectable," added Mr. Hatfield, tone mild. In his mind, he was brokering a business deal, one that made sense for his company's reputation.

"Connor and Alice will have a brief engagement. We'll make sure they are seen on the town hand in hand, wildly in love, to explain the shortened time line. Alice will make a lovely June bride."

"And what of the baby?" Wilhelmina blurted, unable to contain her curiosity. Her hand flew up to her mouth, eyes gone wide with embarrassment. "I apologize, Mr. and Mrs. Hatfield. You owe me no explanation and I did not mean to impose."

"No, dear, it's only natural you'd want to know what will happen to the baby," Mrs. Hatfield said. "Vernon and I will take the baby for the time being. We'll hide him away until after the honeymoon. When they return, we'll put out word that a distant cousin of Connor's has died in a car accident, along with his wife. Connor and Alice will selflessly step up to adopt their infant son and care for him as their own."

"They've thought of everything, my brilliant businessman of a father and socialite mother," Connor said, voice dripping with derision.

"Perhaps if you'd been less careless, we wouldn't have to think of everything. We're lucky we didn't have to figure out what to do with the Satler girl's baby," Mr. Hatfield hissed, his round face becoming ruddy with anger.

Mrs. Hatfield touched his arm, a look on her face that said plainly "not here." Mr. Hatfield seemed to deflate, his chest sinking lower, shoulders rolling into a less imposing posture. Wilhelmina wondered how much of his life Mr. Hatfield spent making himself smaller and less intimidating for the sake of good business.

"Yes, well, Nurse Darrington, now that you understand the situation, could you please help Alice with her things?" Dr. Covington's voice was mild, and he wore a vaguely amused expression that Wilhelmina knew he used when he was trying to remain neutral.

. . .

A little over an hour later, Wilhelmina stood with Alice and the Hatfields in the main entryway. Alice cradled her baby in her arms, smiling and cooing at him as Natalie approached. The two locked eyes, a silent communication passing between them. Wilhelmina turned away from them but couldn't ignore the goosebumps pricking at her arms.

"I've decided to call him Arthur," Alice said. Wilhelmina turned back to the women, taking in Alice's radiant smile and Natalie's rounded eyes. A softness came over Natalie's face, transforming her from haughty beauty to jovial friend. Natalie threw her arms around Alice and the baby, careful not to crush Arthur between them.

"I will never forget you, Alice."

"You'd better not. I expect letters from wherever you land, Natalie."

"I promise."

"Me too."

Alice and Natalie were still staring at each other, eyes shining with sappy tears, when Mr. Hatfield pushed his son forward. Connor hesitated for a moment before settling his hand on Alice's mid-back, guiding her out the door.

"Ladies," Mr. Hatfield said, dipping his head respectfully at Wilhelmina and Natalie.

"Thank you," Mrs. Hatfield said, voice filled with emotion.

Wilhelmina and Natalie watched as Alice settled in the back of the Hatfields' car just as they'd watched when Beatrice had settled into the back of a taxi. It filled Wilhelmina with a sense of contentment to watch the Hatfields' car disappear behind the topiary trees, knowing that Alice would be well cared for.

"Poor thing," Natalie said.

Wilhelmina turned to look at her, mouth open, a furrow between her brows. "She got exactly what she wanted. A comfortable marriage, a father for her child, a stable future. How is that poor?"

"You call being married to a man who doesn't love you comfortable?"

Wilhelmina opened her mouth to respond, closed it, and stared off to the edge of the grounds as though she could still glimpse the car. "People have been marrying for things other than love since the invention of marriage, Natalie. Sometimes it leads to love, sometimes to friendship, and very often to comfort."

"Maybe, maybe not. You're right. Alice got what she wanted. She got to marry the man she hoped had loved her, but didn't. Her baby has a father. She'll live in a comfortable house, and her baby will never want for anything. But she will. She'll want for the love of a husband who will probably never be faithful to her. She's trapped in a dream of her own making." Natalie let out a sigh. "She got what she wanted, but life—"

"—Has a way of balancing itself out." Wilhelmina finished the sentence with Natalie.

Natalie nodded, gave a heavy sigh, and walked away, leaving Wilhelmina to stare out into the grounds, wondering if Natalie was right, and if she was, hoping that the balance was worth it for Alice.

TWENTY

KATIE SLAMMED THE PRINTED PAGES of the journal down on the table with a stifled half-scream groan. Jason peered at her over the top of his laptop, and the students nearest their table jumped and turned startled gazes in their direction. Katie didn't care if the students were staring at her, or if they thought she might be crazy because of her outburst. She stared at the sheet of paper on the top of her stack, the last of the journal scans. *The remaining pages appear to have been torn out before the journal was found.*

"Tell me how you really feel," Jason said, arching a brow.

"I've read the whole thing and all I've got are more questions."

"Okay, well... run what you know by me. Maybe I

can help answer them."

"I know there were three pregnant women here in late 1934, early 1935. I know Wilhelmina walked in on them doing something that scared her. I'm calling it a ritual."

"These are the supposed witches we discussed before in the museum?"

"Yes."

"Alright, if we take what Wilhelmina saw as a ritual, and we assume these women were witches, that gives us three suspects in your curse."

"That's what I think, too."

"Did they do anything else that would give us clues?"

"No... Maybe?"

"Care to elaborate?"

"Well, it's weird. Wilhelmina had these conversations with two of them, about what they wanted. Immediate life goals, you know? And both got it. Like... they just manifested what they wanted."

"Very New Age of them." Jason's voice feigned seriousness, but there was a slight quiver to the corner of his lips.

"I know. It all sounds ridiculous. But one of them talked to Wilhelmina about being powerful and having the power to change her own life. And then what she wanted came to be."

"You think they changed their situations by sheer

force of will?"

"I think it's possible. I think anything is possible at this point."

"You said only two of them had conversations with Wilhelmina. What about the third one?"

"That's the biggest question." Katie slid the stack of papers across the table to Jason. He glanced at the words on the otherwise blank page and looked back up at her with raised eyebrows.

"My gut says it has something to do with that third woman, Natalie. She's the one that made Wilhelmina the most nervous. And I don't know what happened   to   her."

"You think the pages that were ripped out were about her?"

"It's a little too convenient. Maybe they aren't about her. But they were ripped out for a reason, like Wilhelmina didn't want anyone to know what happened in those days."

Jason picked up the stack of pages and fanned them, stopping periodically to read a snippet of Wilhelmina's detailed accounts of her time at Tranquil Heights. Katie watched him look out the window, lost in thought, fanning the papers back and forth in an absent-minded gesture.

"Wilhelmina filled a journal for what, five, six months? A daily recounting of her life. What are the chances she only had this one journal?"

Katie could do nothing but stare at Jason, thoughts spiraling. How had she not thought of the possibility of more journals? It was so obvious, yet it had never even crossed her mind. She picked up her phone, pressed the two, and hit call, her mother's speed dial slot. Jason occupied the first slot.

"Mom, hey." She paused as her mother spoke rapidly on the other end. "Mom, slow down, I'm fine. Everything is fine. I just have a question. Did great-great-grandma Wilhelmina keep journals?"

"Yes."

"What are the odds you've kept them?"

"Pretty high. They're in the attic."

"Great. Jason is going to come get them today."

"There's nothing in them. Your grandmother and I have read them front to back."

"I'd still like to try."

Her mother sighed deeply, then said, "I'll have your father pull them down. They'll be ready for Jason. Katelyn, baby, I understand why you have an obsession with the curse now and why you want to figure it out. But your grandmother and I have been down this road. We've found nothing."

"You never came to Tranquil Heights," Katie said, tone accusatory.

"We did. But it was a graffitied mess overgrown with weeds. There was nothing there to find."

"It's not a graffitied mess anymore, Mom. And I

think I'm getting closer to an answer. At the very least I have more pointed questions to ask. I'm making progress, and I will figure this out."

"That determination and assertiveness, you sound like Liz, not so much like my quiet, introspective Katie."

"I have to fight my own battles now. Liz isn't here to take command, so I will."

"Oh, baby, I'm so sorry."

"Me too, Mom. Me too."

"I love you."

"Love you." The tone that signaled the call disconnected rang in Katie's ear. She set her phone on the table and looked at Jason.

"I'll go now," he said, already packing up his laptop.

"I love you."

"I know."

. . .

Jason attempted to start the car, but the engine made a feeble cranking noise when he turned the key. He cursed under his breath and grabbed his phone from the holder on the dash. He was looking up the phone number for his insurance company when the radio clicked on and a loud static filled the small space. "Jason," a female voice crooned from the speakers.

"What are you chasing?"

Heart racing, Jason yanked the keys from the ignition and pulled the door handle, an act that should have turned off the stereo. Instead, the radio continued to scan. "Believe me, Natalie!" a man's voice said. "Willie, our lives are in your hands," another man's voice called out. "Don't cry, Katie," a third said.

Jason reached for his seat belt release and found it stuck. His door slammed closed and the lock clicked with a finality that made his blood run cold. The sound of the radio scanning grew louder, a static fuzz that made it difficult to think. Jason tugged hard on the seat belt as he frantically searched for something, anything, that could help him. His eyes landed on the glove box where he kept a small first aid kit that included scissors.

He leaned across the center console, arm stretching to its fullest extent, fingers just brushing the glove box. Face flushed with the effort, Jason pulled hard against the chest strap of the seatbelt, trying desperately to gain those last inches that would put the first aid kit in his hand. The seatbelt only locked tighter, and he fell back in his seat with a sharp exhale.

In his hurry to open the door to stop the radio, he'd dropped his phone. He could see it on the floor at his feet, near the gas pedal. He knew it was hopeless to reach for it, but it was synced to the car. He jammed the keys back into the ignition and turned, praying that at the very least he could rely on the car's battery to make a phone call.

To his surprise, the car turned over, engine roaring to life and drowning out the hiss of the radio. The temperature in the car dropped, settling into the bone chilling cold of a winter fog. *Scorpio Rising* by The Mountain Goats blared from the radio.

"Stop digging, stop searching, I get it!" he screamed into the cold air.

A disturbance in the air drew his attention to the passenger seat. If the seat belt hadn't trapped him, he would have flung himself from the vehicle. The woman he had seen during Katie's failed attempt to contact Liz sat in the seat and gazed at him with skin-crawling intensity. An abrupt silence filled the vehicle as the radio turned off. He could hear nothing but the slight wheezing of his own breath as he gulped painfully cold air into his shocked lungs. The woman—ghost—opened her mouth and Jason expected the same ragged, angry scream he'd heard just two nights before.

Instead, a soft sigh slithered through the car to land gently in his ear, like the whisper of a lover. "Go." Jason didn't need to be told twice. He threw the car in gear and peeled out of the parking lot, leaving black streaks on the pavement and curling clouds of smoke. The White Lady had disappeared, and Jason didn't slow down until the tires of his vehicle hit the pavement of the highway, leaving Tranquil Heights behind.

TWENTY-ONE

KATIE WAS SHOVING THE PAGES of the journal into her book bag, paying no mind to creasing and crinkling of the paper, when Darla walked into the dining room. She made a beeline towards Katie as she tugged the zipper on the bag closed and slung it over her head in a rough motion.

"Everything okay?"

"Wha—oh Darla," Katie said, taking a big breath in through her nose and exhaling out of her mouth. "I just got to the end of the journal."

"Ah, the torn pages?"

"Yeah." Katie threw her book bag back into one of the chairs at the table. She pulled out another chair and gestured for Darla to do the same. "It's so disappointing. It's like reading a great thriller novel, only to not get an ending."

"You're not wrong," Darla replied.

"It's just that I had all this buildup of the scary ritual, and then Beatrice and Alice having things work out the way they wanted them to. And then... just nothing."

"I know. I felt the same way the first time I read the journal."

"I didn't get what I needed out of it. I did find out Wilhelmina kept more journals. Jason's gone to my parents' to get them, but I'm not convinced they'll have the answers either."

"What answers are you looking for, exactly? You just told me you wanted to research your family. Maybe I can help?"

Katie weighed her options, eyes on Darla's face. Darla kept eye contact, an expression of pleasant neutrality that conveyed nothing but an honest offer to help. Katie hated the idea of telling anyone else about the family curse, a holdout of the skeptical embarrassment she and Liz had learned while growing up. But Darla knew more than anyone about Tranquil Heights, and that could only be helpful in Katie's quest to figure out how the curse had started.

Katie steeled herself for a negative reaction and told the story of her family. Darla stayed quiet through the whole telling, eyes widening and filling with sadness or confusion at the appropriate moments.

Katie felt lighter, having confided in someone who had no ties to her or her family, and validated because Darla hadn't laughed or scoffed at her.

"So, you're here trying to figure out the origins of the curse to protect your baby?" Darla confirmed after taking a moment to gather her thoughts.

Katie nodded and felt something tickle her cheek. She brushed at it with her hand and was surprised to come away with wet fingers. She hadn't realized that she had cried a steady stream of tears while she told her story. She hadn't cried as much as she supposed she should have since Liz's death. She had thrown herself into figuring out the curse and put everything else, every other thought and feeling, on the back burner.

If she stopped, she'd have to think about the night Liz died. She'd have to think about the fact that she and Jason should have taken Liz home instead of calling her an Uber. And if they had, maybe Liz wouldn't have been on Sixth Street when that beam fell, and maybe she'd still be alive.

If she stopped, she'd have to think about all the times their mother and grandmother had warned them about the curse, how even after she'd outgrown the scary fables and stories, a thrill of fear still ran down her spine at the mention of the family curse. She'd have to think about how she let Liz convince her that curses, ghosts, and magic weren't real, even though she'd always questioned the validity of her sister's assertions.

If she stopped, she would have to think about how it had been easier to just follow Liz to the ends of the earth rather than investigating things and coming to answers on her own. And if she had bothered to think for herself, she would have followed her curiosity to Tranquil Heights before she and Liz turned twenty five. Katie couldn't stop chasing ghosts at Tranquil Heights, because if she did, she'd have to face the reality that if she had made different choices in her life, Liz would still be alive.

"Okay, tell me what you have figured out, so we can figure out what you're missing," Darla said. Her face had softened, but that was the only sign she gave that she noticed Katie's tears. Katie was thankful for Darla's focus. She'd have fallen apart if Darla tried to feel sorry for her.

"I know the curse had to do with a patient here, that much Wilhelmina told her granddaughter, my grandmother. Based on the journal, I think there's a good chance it was Beatrice, Alice, or Natalie. Of course, her daughter was only two then and died at twenty five, so it could have happened any time in between."

"True. So why do you think it was one of our three ladies in this journal?"

"I think for a while, it was just because I wanted

it to be. Because it was easy to bury myself in this journal and try to interpret any and everything as an answer."

"For a while?"

"Yes. My mom has other journals. So why was this one left behind? What's special about it? Why was it hidden in the floorboards?"

"I see your point."

"Plus, I just have this weird gut feeling. I can't explain it, I just feel like I'm close."

"I've learned to trust those feelings, for what it's worth."

"Yeah, I think I'm learning that, too."

"There's nothing specific in the journals that points to any one person."

"No. Again, my gut lands on Natalie. Probably only because Wilhelmina explained being the most afraid of her. But I don't have any specific events that make Natalie more likely than the other two. I don't even know what happened to Natalie."

"I do."

"What!?"

"Well, I don't entirely know. But there's a headstone in the cemetery with her name on it."

"Will you take me to it?"

"Of course."

.   .   .

The cemetery was a short walk from the courtyard. A trail little use in recent years and was partially grown over led to it. An extensive field stretched before them, dotted with old standing headstones. Katie could see more than one intricately carved crying angel, stone pockmarked with holes and green moss after so much time in the elements.

"Due to the nature of Tranquil Heights, it's not a traditional sanitarium or asylum graveyard. For much of the life of the hospital, it was private pay. The families had the money to spend on lavish grave markers. No one would move the TB victims to family plots for fear of catching consumption, so they buried the dead here," Darla explained as they walked.

The grounds of the cemetery weren't as cared for as the rest of the property. Spring in Washington could be brutal when it came to the speed at which grass grew, and no one had mowed the cemetery in at least two weeks. Weeds were taking hold of headstones and choking out the wildflowers that lined the perimeter of the cemetery. Darla stopped in front of a plain-looking headstone, and Katie squatted to pull a creeping vine away from the inscription.

Natalie Arthur, Loyal Friend, Born 14 May 1910, Died 14 May 1935

Katie felt her stomach drop and fell back on her butt in the grass. Goosebumps crept up her arms and sweat broke out on her scalp as she continued to stare at the headstone. "Twenty five," she whispered. "She died exactly on her twenty-fifth birthday."

"I think you've found your patient," Darla said, placing a firm hand on Katie's shoulder.

TWENTY-TWO

TRANQUIL HEIGHTS
PRESENT DAY

"I NEED TO FIGURE OUT HOW SHE DIED," Katie said. She was sitting in a plush chair in her and Jason's room, picking at a string that had come loose in the arm.

"We need to stop digging," Jason said from his spot on the bed. He lay on his back at the foot of the bed, feet flat on the floor and a damp washcloth over his eyes.

"Jason, you know we can't just stop looking."

"The hell we can't." He sat up and fixed Katie with a serious gaze. He was still pale, face a kind of ashy gray that concerned her. "You weren't there. My life was in danger. If we keep looking, it's not just potentially the life of the baby on the line."

"Jason, your life wasn't in danger. Nothing happened to you except the radio acting spooky and your seat belt being stuck. Seat belts get stuck all the time."

"She was in the car with me, Katie!"

"I know, Jason, I know. She's been in room 302 with us more than once, too." Katie's eyes grew wide, and she smacked her palm to her forehead before launching herself out of the chair and to the desk where she rifled through the pages of the journal. "Right here! I don't know why I didn't realize before. Natalie's room was room 302."

"You think Natalie is The White Lady?" Darla said. She had been watching Katie and Jason argue quietly from her spot on the floor, head swiveling back and forth as though at a tennis match.

"That's a big conclusion to jump to," Katie admitted, "but I've spent my time here jumping to bigger conclusions. I've jumped to the conclusion that Natalie is the patient who was involved in my family's curse. It's all based on cosmic coincidences with no actual proof."

"Oh, good. *Now* you admit to everything being coincidences and having no proof. I've only been keeping my mouth shut about my skepticism this whole trip because I thought you working through this was you working through your grief. I didn't actually think we'd find witches or black magic or whatever the fuck you want to call this shit. But NOW, after a ghost showed up in the car with me and told me to stop looking into this, you say you have no actual proof. THE PROOF WAS IN THE CAR WITH ME, KATIE!" Jason's voice rose several octaves, and a light sheen of sweat glistened on his forehead.

"Jason, deep breaths." Katie crossed the room and hugged his head to her chest, placing her cheek to his dark hair. "I know what happened today was terrifying. A lot of stuff that's happened here has been terrifying. And it's worse for you because you've never believed in ghosts or anything remotely paranormal. Your entire understanding of the world has been blown to pieces in the last two days."

Jason raised his head, eyes boring into Katie's. "This is insane."

"Yeah, it is," Katie said, half laughing. "But we'll get through it. Together, we can make it through anything."

Jason drew in a deep breath and exhaled loudly. He rolled his shoulders back, posture returning to the proud and open way he carried himself under normal circumstances. A familiar expression of stubborn determination took over his face, and a wide smile took hold of her own. They continued to look at each other, communicating in a way that only significant others can. A movement caught their attention and reminded them that there was more in the world than just the two of them. Darla was almost to the door, watching them, a deer caught in headlights.

"Sorry, I just thought maybe you didn't need an audience for," she waved her hand out in front of her, gesturing at them. "All that."

A flush crept up Katie's cheeks, and Jason barked a laugh before pulling Katie down to sit next to him on the foot of the bed.

Katie batted at him playfully, eyes twinkling with humor despite the brilliant red of her cheeks. "I'm sorry, Darla. I didn't mean to make this awkward for you."

"I'm sorry, too. You should stay. We have brainstorming to do," Jason said, giving a confident nod. "What about checking newspaper clippings?"

Darla settled into the plush armchair. "No dice. She was being hidden here by a politician with a lot of money. The only thing that would have been posted was an obituary with little information, and I doubt there would even be that."

"Patient records?" Katie asked.

"They would likely have the truth in them. But they aren't public record, and I don't have the passwords to get to the scanned records."

Katie deflated, shoulders hunched in towards her chest, head hung low. "This can't be it. We've accepted the reality of a curse, we've hauled ourselves out here, been accosted by a ghost. This can't be the end of the road."

"Well... there is one more thing I can think of,"

Darla said, voice guarded. Jason and Katie looked at her, afraid to ask. "We could break into the physical records storage in the basement."

"That's crazy," Katie responded, shaking her head.

"This whole thing is crazy," Jason chided.

The three of them sat in silence, measuring each other for commitment and bravery. Slowly, each one of them smiled, then began a slow rumble of laughter, then each one of them rolled to the floor, laughing so hard tears streamed from their eyes.

. . .

"I don't know why I thought this was a good idea," Jason hissed from his place behind Katie. Darla was ahead of them, leading them through a door at the back of the rec room. It was past midnight. They had waited an hour past the students' curfew to ensure they wouldn't be spotted. Still, they each had donned outfits of black or other dark colors. Katie felt as though she were starring in a heist movie.

"None of us thought it was a *good* idea," Darla whispered back.

Katie nodded. "I believe the exact word we used was 'crazy.'"

Katie and Jason peered past Darla's shoulders down a long white hallway, walls relieved by the indents of many doors. Katie had the sudden vision of Wilhelmina walking down this hallway, spooked by the sounds of Natalie, Alice, and Beatrice sneaking into the common room to perform whatever ritual they'd done on Christmas Eve in 1934. The three of them crept forward towards the door at the end of the hallway that Darla explained led to the basement.

"Shit!" Darla said, voice low, but still echoing down the empty hallway.

"What is it?" Jason asked.

"They've put a padlock on the door. Last time I was down there, the door was open, but the filing cabinets were locked. Breaking a filing cabinet lock is easy. A padlock, not so much."

"Okay, spread out and find something that can help us pick the lock," Jason said, slipping into leadership in a way that told Darla that he was used to being in charge. Darla raised eyebrows at him, the question left hanging in the air between them. "I wasn't always the professional Boy Scout. I've got some tricks up my sleeve." His smile was broad and gleaming in the dark, and Katie stifled a laugh.

"Okay, Mr. Commando," Darla teased as she drifted to the first door on the right. Katie took the door on the left, and Jason proceeded to the next door on the right.

They methodically moved room to room, looking for anything that could help. They met in the middle of the hallway, each showing a handful of paper clips, letter openers, and even a set of keys that Katie had found in a desk drawer. Jason was picking through the options when a loud thunk echoed through the hall. Their heads snapped up, pulses speeding, sweat gluing their shirts to their backs. Katie pointed silently to the door to the common room where a flickering light cast dancing shadows on the floor from beneath the door. She and Darla locked eyes, both thinking of Wilhelmina's experience in this very hallway. A tugging at Katie's sleeve turned her to look at the other end of the hall, where Jason was pointing.

There, hanging from the large D-ring, was the padlock, open and swinging. Goosebumps ran up Katie's arms in painful waves. Darla rubbed her arms, and Jason shuddered next to her. Katie could taste the copper tang of blood at the back of her throat, and it occurred to her it was what fear tasted like. They crept forward toward the door to the basement, pressed together in long lines from shoulder to thigh.

"The only way in is through the rec room door," Darla breathed, voice barely audible above Katie's frantically beating heart.

"We would have seen or heard someone come through," Katie replied.

"Well, we came here to get a record. Best not to look a gift horse in the mouth. Or would that be gift ghost?" Jason said mildly.

Katie took a deep breath as Darla let out a nervous giggle. Katie knew Darla saw Jason as calm and in charge. He was, but she also knew his coping mechanism was humor. He was just as terrified as she and Darla, he just hid it better.

Jason cocked his head as if to say, "do we move on?" Katie and Darla looked at each other, took deep breaths, and nodded in unison.

The stairwell was impossibly dark. Jason pulled his phone from his pocket and turned on the flashlight, granting a five-foot swell of light that showed them the stairs. They made their way down, still huddled together, ears straining for any hint of company. A collective sigh of relief left them when their feet hit the concrete floor of the basement. Jason swung the flashlight out into the large room.

"The filing cabinets are along the back wall," Darla explained.

They moved deeper into the cavernous room, jumping at shadows as Jason's flashlight slid over old furniture and broken fixtures. Katie gasped when she glimpsed something tall covered by a white sheet. She laughed at herself when Jason had brought the flashlight around quickly to where she pointed.

"I'm sorry. I thought it was The White Lady." She could see the shine of Darla's eyes as she nodded. "Basements are already creepy enough without being in haunted former asylums."

The room was big enough that Katie expected their voices to echo like they had in the hallway upstairs. But between the furniture, the sheets, and the years of dust, their chuckles left their mouths and disappeared into a strange nothingness that spooked Katie more than the echoes would have.

They stopped in front of a wall of filing cabinets. Katie walked along them, eyes on the alphabet labels. When she came to the drawer labeled "Aq-Az," she reached out to the handle without thinking, yanking on the drawer. It was locked, as Darla had said it would be, but Katie still felt a small sense of disappointment.

Jason moved forward, armed with unfolded paper clips. He gave Katie a reassuring smile and set to work at the tiny lock on the cabinet drawer. Katie held her breath as she watched him work and only let it out when she heard the audible click of the drawer unlocking.

"Still got it," Jason said, grinning broadly. Katie laughed and shook her head as she stepped back up to the filing cabinet.

Katie opened the drawer, the sliding sound of metal-on-metal deafening in the otherwise silent space. Sweat tickled down her back in streams, and she had to take deep breaths to calm the shaking in her hands. The knowledge in these files felt powerful to Katie, and she wasn't sure if they or she had caused the tingling sensation at the base of her skull.

Her hands quickly ran over old files, eyes searching for Natalie's name. A thrill ran up her spine as she spotted an old and tattered blue file. She yanked it from the drawer, breath coming fast with anticipation. She opened the folder, and Darla and Jason watched her face fall, eyes filling with tears. The folder fluttered to the ground, Katie's hands frozen in front of her as though she were still holding it.

Jason and Darla looked down at the ground. The blue folder labeled *Arthur, Natalie* lay open upon the dusty floor, empty.

TWENTY-THREE

KATIE'S EYES BURNED WITH EXHAUSTION. She, Jason, and Darla had come back to her and Jason's room and sat in dejected silence. The three of them had stared at the walls, wracking their brains for answers, limbs heavy with disappointment and fatigue. They'd each drifted off to a restless sleep but woke with the sun just after five in the morning. Jason had moved to the in-room coffee pot, making a strong, dark brew that tickled Katie's nose.

"I'm even more convinced that it's Natalie at this point," Katie said, voice still thick with sleep.

"How so?" Jason asked, pouring the coffee in three mugs.

"The pages missing from the journal, her records being empty. Someone didn't want anyone to know what happened to Natalie. Why hide it if it isn't horrible?"

"That's fair. But what does that really have to do with the curse?"

Katie sighed. "Look, I can't be sure. What I do know is that Wilhelmina said it had something to do with a patient. She kept meticulous journals about her time her and the interactions with those patients. Alice, Beatrice, and Natalie had some kind of power, something Wilhelmina could sense, and it spooked her. We know what happened to Alice and Beatrice, which leaves Natalie. But the pages are gone. She wouldn't tell my grandmother anything about the curse. This journal was hidden here... in the floorboard of Natalie's room, when all the other journals are in those boxes." She pointed at the stacks of document boxes Jason had retrieved from her parents' house.

Jason raised his hands, waving a proverbial white flag. "You're right. It does seem like everything is pointing to Natalie. So," he gestured to the document boxes. "We start there. We find whatever we can in these other journals."

Katie's mother hadn't lied when she'd said they had already read all the journals. They'd organized them by date, each box holding a different year. Hundreds of journals in dozens of boxes, documenting every facet of Wilhelmina Darrington's life. Katie scanned the boxes, looking for the one with dates directly after the journal they had. She finally found a box labeled 1935-1936 and shifted two boxes off of it, pulling it out to the center of the room. Jason and Darla stood over her, watching over her shoulders as she lifted the lid from the box.

Katie looked down at a crocheted afghan, put together from so many colors and types of yarn that it was dizzying to look at. Katie pulled it gingerly from the box, afraid that it may fall apart due to its advanced age and potential damage from critters. It was perfectly preserved, and Katie wrinkled her nose at the smell of the mothballs she could see on the edges of the box filled with journals.

"What's the deal with the blanket?" Jason asked.

"No idea," Katie replied.

"Well, she kept it with the journals until the day she died. It must have been important to her."

"Yeah. Let's see if we can find out why," Katie said as she dug into the box, handing journals to both Jason and Darla.

They each took up post in different parts of the room: Darla, curled in the chair, legs tucked up under her; Jason sitting on the bed, back up against the headboard; Katie at the desk, journal lying flat on the surface. The room was silent, the only sound the ticking of a clock on the wall, and the only movement the swirling dance of the dust in the slivers of sunlight peeking through the curtains.

"I think I have the book just after the journal that was found here," Darla said. "It starts on June 1, 1935. Wilhelmina says: 'Violet has not been back to work in two weeks. Dr. Covington told me that her mother said Violet is quite ill. I think it's more likely she's sick of heart. So am I. What we saw that night was a nightmare come to life. It haunts my dreams. Bradley shakes me awake most nights because I am screaming, the sheets twisted around my body and soaked with sweat. I will never recover from what I have seen, and neither will Violet. Though I understand why she hasn't set foot back at Tranquil Heights, I hope she comes back. I miss her. And she is the only person I can talk to about what happened, the only person who witnessed the horror. The only person who could understand my guilt.'"

"Well, that's heavy," Jason said, his own journal laying open in his lap.

"Whatever happened, it had a profound impact on Wilhelmina, and it sounds like Violet as well," Katie agreed.

"She goes on to talk about Natalie's mother, listen: 'Mrs. Arthur came today. I sat with her in a little waiting room while Dr. Covington collected the funeral payment from Senator Cumberland. Mrs. Arthur is a widow and doesn't have the money to arrange for proper services off the grounds of Tranquil

Heights. She hadn't even known that Natalie was here. She still doesn't know why Natalie was here, and it pains me to not be able to tell her about her grandchild. While we sat, she told me stories from Natalie's childhood. I wanted her to stop, but I couldn't say anything. I sat there in silence while Mrs. Arthur told me that Natalie was her firstborn, the oldest of four girls. She told me that Natalie was the leader, and the other three will be lost without her. I am unsurprised that she was the leader. And even more gutted to know more about the family who will miss her desperately.'"

"The firstborn daughter, dead at twenty five," Jason said, eyebrows high on his forehead. Katie could only nod in response, thoughts on Liz, and how she was pretty sure she understood how Natalie's sisters must have felt. They fell again into silence.

Thirty minutes passed when Darla again spoke up, reading from her journal, "June 30th, 1935 'Violet has finally returned. She is thinner than she was. Her body used to still hold that chubbiness that some teenagers hold on to from childhood. She is now long and lean, her cheeks just a little too drawn. We ate together in silence. She confirmed my suspicions, that she wasn't so much physically ill as emotionally ill. It had physical consequences, of course. She couldn't eat, could barely sleep. She told me she keeps replaying that night over and over again in her head, trying to determine if there was something more we could have done. She says she sees the ground outside the window whenever she closes her eyes. So do I.'"

This time an hour passed before Jason sat up a little straighter. "This is from December 24, 1935 'I found myself in the common room. I'm not even sure how I got here. I just was suddenly standing in the doorway off the medical hallway, watching last Christmas Eve play out in front of me all over again. Beatrice and Alice look like memories, sort of hazy, fuzzy around the edges like my memory is failing, just a little. But Natalie, she looks real. Everything about her is in sharp focus, almost like she has a spotlight shone on only her. Like last Christmas, the room was hot, and the air felt heavy. Natalie just stared at me, those icy blue eyes at odds with the heat of the room. I apologized to her. I couldn't stop the words from falling from my lips. I told her I knew everything was my fault. That if only I had been just a little braver, she'd still be among the living, cooing over her beautiful daughter.'"

"You think Wilhelmina saw her as The White Lady that night?" Katie asked.

"I think it's possible," Jason replied before returning his eyes to the book.

Most of the day passed with nothing more interesting. In 1936, Wilhelmina stopped mentioning Natalie, or "that night." The three of them moved through box after box of journals, a boring account of Wilhelmina's life. Katie lay on the floor under the desk, a journal from 1957 open in front of her. She sat up so quickly, she smacked her head hard on the underside of the desk but moved quickly out from under it, eyes streaming, journal gripped tightly in her hands.

"December 5, 1957 'Today, Eleanor turned twenty five. She has blossomed into a radiant woman. She is an excellent mother. Her daughters, Mary and Virginia, are precious and smart. Having grandchildren is a delight. I loved watching them help blow out their mother's candles on her cake. It would have been a perfect day if I could have avoided thinking about Natalie. I opened the box in which I keep the afghan I made her this morning. She was only twenty five when her life was cut short, just like my Eleanor. I thought of Mrs. Arthur, who told me all about her first born daughter, the light of her family. Natalie had so much more to offer the world, so much power to change the world. I rarely allow myself to think of her. It's too painful. I am filled with guilt. It is my fault that her life ended so abruptly. I ended her life at only twenty five. I took everything from her. I broke Mrs. Arthur's family, cast her other daughters adrift. I do not deserve the happiness I have with my daughter and grandchildren. None of us deserve this kind of happiness.' And then December 6, 1957. 'The police knocked on my door just past midnight, the red and blue of their lights carving strange shapes out of the living room furniture. Eleanor and her husband rented a hotel room for the night, Bradley and I kept the girls. Shortly after eleven last night, after a night of champagne and dancing, Eleanor lost her footing on the balcony of their hotel room. She fell over the railing. She is dead. Dead at twenty five, just like Natalie. Because I was right. We do not deserve this happiness in the face of what I've done.'"

"My god, what did she do to Natalie that she thinks she deserved to have her daughter die?" Jason asked.

"I dunno," Katie replied, flipping and scanning the next few pages. "She gives no detail."

Silence stretched again until they were on the last box late in the afternoon. They read reading slower, exhaustion catching up with them, eyes weary from reading for so many hours.

"February 17th, 1967 'The time has come for me to retire. I don't want to, but my body is slowing down. I find it difficult to remain on my feet on these hard floors. The standard of care in this place has fallen to a point that it is unpalatable to me. I don't imagine it will be open much longer. Even so, I don't want to leave. I can feel Natalie everywhere I go on these grounds. Sometimes it's just a tickle of warm wind in a room with closed windows. Sometimes it's a humid pocket so fierce, I feel as though I may drown. And sometimes, at night, when everyone else is asleep, I swear I can see her walking the halls, the grounds, staring up at the window of room 302. She's here, I know it. And I can't bring myself to leave when she's stuck here forever, alone and devastated as she was the day she died. Some piece of me shall always remain here, I think, even after I no longer physically come here.'" Jason dropped the journal he was holding into his lap. "This is the last entry in that journal, and the last journal we have. She stopped keeping them after she retired."

"We're no closer to an answer," Katie said as she sighed, snapping her journal closed and setting it down.

"No, but I think you're right. I think Natalie is the key to this whole thing."

"But we have no way of finding out what happened to her." Katie got up from the floor and crossed to him, one hand resting on her stomach, the other finding one of his large hands. "We're at a dead end. We can't figure out the origins of this curse."

Katie stood next to the bed in their room at Tranquil Heights, cradling the unborn child she was convinced would be a daughter as she held her husband's hand and openly wept.

TWENTY-FOUR

KATIE COULD HEAR A HEAVY THUMPING NOISE and lifted her head groggily from the pillow. Jason groaned in her ear and pulled her tighter against his chest. Her eyes felt achy and tired. She'd cried late into the night, devastated by what appeared to the be the end of the road for her breaking her family's curse. The thumping noise continued, followed by a woman's voice.

"Edgecombs! Wake up! I have news!"

Katie glanced at the clock. It was only 7:32, and the two nights of little sleep weighed heavily on her. But she moved Jason's arm off her and slipped out from between the covers. Jason sighed and sat up, hair sticking up in wild directions, deep shadows under his eyes.

"Darla, this better be good," Katie said as she opened the door.

"It is!" Darla crowed, bounding into the room with far too much energy. "I found her!"

"Found who?"

"Violet Brown!"

Katie stared blankly at Darla for several long moments. Darla's face was shining, alight with excitement. Her whole body appeared to be vibrating. Katie felt the pieces click together, the puzzle building itself in her mind's eye.

"Oh my god! Wait, but Violet Brown must be, what, 101 by now?"

"102, actually," Darla replied. "I couldn't sleep last night, and I've been working on this project in the museum, making a wall thanking all the donors. And it just flashed in my brain, there's a woman named Violet that contributes to the museum every year. So I've done some digging and," Darla waved a sheet of paper in front of Katie's face. "Violet Brown became Violet Camden, and she's been donating to the museum since it opened. She even comes in and speaks during scheduled tours sometimes. I just never put together who she was until now."

Katie rushed Darla, throwing her arms around her newfound friend and jumping up and down, forcing Darla to jump with her.

Darla laughed and extricated herself from Katie's

grip, placing the paper in Katie's hands. "I've found her address. How would you like to pay a visit to Violet Camden?"

. . .

Two and a half hours later, Katie, Jason, and Darla stood on the sidewalk in front of a quaint house in the uptown of Port Townsend. Katie and Jason had dressed in a rush and met Darla in the parking lot. They'd only just made it to the Edmonds-Kingston ferry in time to load and cross the Sound to the Peninsula.

Katie looked from Darla to Jason, who both nodded at her, and she moved up the sidewalk to knock on the red door.

A young woman answered, probably about Katie's age. "Can I help you?" she said, eyes glancing over Katie, to Darla and Jason behind her. "Hi. My name is Katie. I'm looking for Violet Camden. My great-great-grandmother Wilhelmina used to work with her at Tranquil Heights, and I was hoping I could ask her some questions about their time there."

The young woman narrowed her eyes and closed the door. Katie could see through the window in the door that she had retreated further in the house. Katie looked at Jason, eyebrows raised, wondering what she should do, when the young woman opened the door again.

"Please, come in. My great-grandmother says she's been expecting you." She stepped back from the door and motioned the trio into the house.

A rush of excitement unsettled Katie's stomach as she crossed the threshold. She caught Jason's eye and saw the same question reflected in his eyes. How did Violet Camden know about Katie, and why had she been expecting her?

The young woman led them into a comfortable sitting room off the kitchen where an old woman with snow white hair and a kind face sat in a rocking chair. Katie thought that Violet Camden looked like a television grandmother. All she was missing was a storybook and a cast of puppets.

Katie stepped forward and introduced herself to Violet. She noted the soft papery feeling of her skin as she shook her hand. She didn't look like she was 102, but the skin gave away the age of the woman in the rocking chair.

"You have her eyes," Violet said to her, a sad smile touching her lips.

"My sister, Liz, looked just like her," Katie said, pulling her phone from her pocket and showing Violet a photo of her and Liz from the birthday party.

Violet's eyes filled with tears as she took in the photo, and Katie gave her a moment to remember her friend. "You said your sister looked just like her,"

Violet said, emphasizing the "ed" in "looked." "I suppose that's why you're here?"

"Yes, ma'am. My sister died about a month ago on our twenty-fifth birthday." Katie looked down at her phone, taking deep, shaky breaths. She'd have time to fall apart about the loss of Liz so many times in the future. But now, she had a mystery to solve.

Jason set his hand on her shoulder, and Katie nodded, letting him know she would be okay.

"Truth be told, I expected someone from your family sooner."

"Older generations tried, but Wilhelmina was determined to keep the origins of the curse a secret. And Tranquil Heights wasn't restored, and the museum not started until well into the 2000s. I think my mom and grandma had given up and didn't realize that Tranquil Heights the prep school might offer answers."

"At any rate, I'm glad you're here." Violet turned to look at her great-granddaughter. "Annie, honey, there is an old envelope in my vanity drawer in my bedroom. It's addressed to Violet Brown from Wilhelmina Darrington. Will you bring it to me, please?"

Katie's stomach rolled as Annie left the room and returned with an envelope, yellowed with age. Annie placed the envelope in Violet's hands and the older woman pulled several sheets of paper from the envelope.

"When Willy retired, she sent me this letter and a collection of journal pages. They should explain everything. At least as much as this can be explained." Violet held the pages out to Katie.

Katie's hand shook as she took the pages. The letter was on a beautiful, floral stationary, written in the handwriting she recognized as Wilhelmina's. The other pages were smaller and matched the pages in the journal on display in the museum. Katie looked at Violet, who nodded at her, the same sad smile on her face. Katie looked at the letter and read it aloud for Jason and Darla.

February 17, 1967

Dear Vi,

I'm retiring, and I can hardly believe it. All these years I haven't told a soul what happened to Natalie. And I want to keep it that way. You are the only other living being who knows exactly what happened that night. I can't bear for anyone else to know. I've enclosed the last pages of my journal, the ones that describe that night and the events that led up to it. I think it would do some irreparable damage to destroy them, but I can't explain why I feel that way. And it's not as though I haven't already done irreparable damage with Natalie.

I know we haven't spoken since my Eleanor died, and for that I apologize. I hid away from everyone at that point, so great was my sadness. And my guilt. I don't believe that Eleanor will be the last. I think my family may be doomed. Natalie had so much potential cut off at twenty five, all because I was not brave enough to stand up for her. Because I was selfish and afraid of losing my job. She didn't deserve what happened to her. And I could have changed the course of everything that happened.

I can't tell you why, but I am sure that what happened to Eleanor will happen again. I think many daughters in my family will lose their lives senselessly at twenty five. Because I cut Natalie's life short at twenty five. And as Natalie always said, life has a way of balancing itself. This is the balance. This the penance I and my family must pay for my selfish cowardice.

I refuse to tell my grandchildren about Natalie. I have only told them to be prepared that it is likely the firstborn daughter in each generation will only have twenty-five years to make a difference on this planet. I cannot—will not—tell them why. They will only try to stop it from happening. And stopping it could only further disrupt the balance of life. I cannot imagine how much worse things could get if I do not just accept the balance life has brought down upon me and mine.

Keep this secret for me, my friend.

I love you.

Wilhelmina Darrington

TWENTY-FIVE

WILHELMINA HAD TAKEN TO WALKING the grounds with Natalie in the evenings. With Alice gone, they were both a little lonely and had built a comfortable friendship, despite the unease with which they'd treated each other only months before. The days were growing longer, and the weather was dry more often than not, though the evenings were still chilly. Wilhelmina held her sweater closed, guarding herself against the chill as she and Natalie rounded the gazebo in the courtyard. They'd celebrated Natalie's twenty-fifth birthday that day in the common room, though her birthday wasn't until the next day. Natalie had asked to celebrate early because she had been sure the baby would be born the next day and would have ruined the festivities. Wilhelmina had crocheted her a small afghan, a patchwork of competing colors that had come from Wilhelmina's ever-growing stash of yarn remnants. Natalie held it around her shoulders.

"Would you like to stop and sit in the gazebo for a while?" Wilhelmina asked Natalie, who was so heavily pregnant that she didn't so much walk as waddle.

Natalie waved her off and continued down the gravel path. "No stopping, Willy. This baby is overcooked as it is. I am determined to walk it right out of me."

"It'll come when it's ready."

"As long as it's ready before next Thursday, that's fine."

Much to Wilhelmina's shock, an envelope had come addressed to Natalie from Senator Cumberland. The envelope had contained only a one-way ticket to Philadelphia. No note, no explanation. Natalie had crowed with excitement and hugged Wilhelmina tight to her. Wilhelmina had spoken to Dr. Covington, as she'd promised, and he had agreed that it was better not to steal children away from mothers who would love and care for them. He'd promised to speak with senator Cumberland but held as much hope as Wilhelmina did that the senator would agree.

Her pleasant surprise was torn away when Dr. Covington had pulled her into his office the next day upon her arrival at work. He handed a letter to her and sat down heavily behind his desk. It was a letter addressed to Dr. Covington from Senator Cumberland. In it he stated he agreed it was best if Natalie didn't remain in the Seattle area, but under no circumstances was she to keep the baby. Wilhelmina's shoulders had sagged and she felt the hot pinpricks of tears threatening to form as she handed the letter back to the doctor.

"I'm just as disappointed as you are, Wilhelmina." Dr. Covington handed a handkerchief across the desk to her. She could only nod as she blotted the handkerchief at her eyes, afraid that her voice would betray just how devastated she was on Natalie's behalf. "There's more, Wilhelmina."

"Lord have mercy." Wilhelmina choked out a bitter laugh. "When it rains, it pours."

"I think we should keep this news from Ms. Arthur."

"Dr. Covington, she's so excited, we can't possibly—"

"It is precisely her excitement that makes me say we shouldn't tell her. She is very close to being due. I don't want any upset to jeopardize her or the baby at this point."

Wilhelmina took a deep breath and nodded, though she struggled to meet his eyes. She understood his reasoning and even agreed with it to a certain extent. She also didn't want to have to look into

Natalie's heartbroken face upon her receipt of the news.

"It's unfair, Dr. Covington. Natalie's entire life, her reputation, everything is ruined. And in a few months' time Senator Cumberland will sit in the governor's mansion without a dent in his sterling reputation. You know Natalie didn't even go to his bed willingly? He is entirely responsible for her situation, and he loses nothing." Wilhelmina stood up and started pacing, unable to contain her anger in a still body.

"I am aware of the more... unsavory pieces of Natalie's situation, Wilhelmina. And you are right, it isn't fair. But this is simply the way the world works. What would you have of me?"

"Willy?" Natalie said.

Wilhelmina blinked several times, clearing her mind of the memory of Senator Cumberland's cruelty. She looked at Natalie who stood a few paces ahead on the gravel path in the courtyard. She shook her shoulders, attempting to rid herself of the negativity the way a dog rids its coat of water after the rain. She smiled at Natalie, though she could feel the smile didn't meet her eyes.

"Sorry, I was busy making a grocery list in my head." Wilhelmina closed the distance between herself and Natalie, and Natalie gave her a puzzled look as she turned back to continue walking. Raised brows replaced furrowed brows, and her mouth formed a round "O" shape as she looked down at the ground. The gravel below Natalie was dark and shining with liquid, and a small laugh bubbled out from between Natalie's lips.

"I guess this baby heard me loud and clear about coming out," she said, face shining with happiness. Wilhelmina gripped Natalie's elbow and started leading her back towards the primary building. "Happy birthday to me!"

. . .

Four hours later, Wilhelmina was placing a cool, damp cloth across Natalie's forehead. Sweat pasted Natalie's blonde hair to her head, and her blue eyes shone with pain. Wilhelmina's hand was beginning to show bruises in the shape of Natalie's fingers, but she was ready to grip the woman's hand once again.

"Okay, Natalie, we're almost there. Give me one more big push." Dr. Covington's voice came from beyond the blanket covering Natalie's knees.

Natalie pushed herself up on her elbows, teeth bared, hand clamped around Wilhelmina's. She screamed as she bared down, and Wilhelmina wasn't sure if she'd ever be able to hear out of that ear again. A wavering cry sounded from the bottom of the bed and Natalie fell back, exhausted, but laughing.

"It's a girl! Born 12:32am on May the 14th, 1935." Dr. Covington shouted. Orderlies were deftly wrapping the pink baby in a blanket. Dr. Covington met Wilhelmina's eyes over the top of Natalie's bed, his lips set in a tight, closed smile. He took a deep breath and nodded to the orderly who laid the baby in Natalie's arms. "We'll give you some time," he said, more to Wilhelmina than to Natalie. Wilhelmina knew he meant to give Natalie time to drink in the curves of the baby's tiny face, her little toes and fingers, before someone came to take the baby to the orphanage.

Wilhelmina stayed in the room, taking up post in a chair next to the bed to watch Natalie fall in love with her baby. She'd had an orderly call home for her just after eleven to inform her husband that she wouldn't be home for several hours. She had the time to stay and see this through. Though Natalie didn't know what was to happen, Wilhelmina knew she was strong and would survive this. And if Natalie could survive having that bundle taken from her, then Wilhelmina could survive watching th young woman fall in love with her daughter knowing what was to happen.

Wilhelmina still sat there two hours later, watching Natalie, who had succumbed to her exhaustion and slept soundly, the baby laying in a cradle next to the bed. Justin, the orderly, entered the room quietly. His eyes met Wilhelmina's, and he shrugged, holding his hands out in front of him. He asked silently, "What am I supposed to do? These are my orders." Wilhelmina nodded even as a weight settled on her chest and tears sprang to her eyes. Justin rolled the cradle out the door so carefully that the baby never stirred.

It was only thirty minutes more until Natalie woke, casting a bleary-eyed gaze about the room, searching for her baby. She rubbed the sleep from her eyes and settled her gaze on Wilhelmina. She gave Wilhelmina a sleepy smile, a few watts short of her most brilliant, and pushed herself up into a sitting position to look more thoroughly around the room. "Where is she?"

"Natalie... the senator—"

"He did NOT change his mind. He can't." Natalie's voice grew by several octaves.

"He didn't. He never agreed to you keeping the baby. He only agreed that you should leave."

"Wilhelmina Darrington, where is my baby?"

"They have taken her to the orphanage, as the senator demanded," Wilhelmina said in a hushed voice, unable to meet Natalie's eyes.

Natalie's wail was so great that Wilhelmina was sure the glass in the windows would shatter.

. . .

Wilhelmina made her usual rounds when she returned to Tranquil Heights later that same day. She checked in at the nurse's station near the back entry and read through the notes the day nurse left. They had sent Violet to keep Natalie company. Natalie was refusing to leave her room and had taken both of her meals in there, though Violet had noted she had eaten nothing from those two meals.

Wilhelmina was unsurprised by anything regarding Natalie and continued with her daily routine of checking in with other patients. She administered medications that needed to be taken with food to patients in the dining room at dinner time and helped the orderlies observe the mealtime, there to help if anything got out of hand.

Wilhelmina was closing down the common room at quarter to eleven, turning off the TV and returning board game pieces to their respective boxes. The patients had a habit of retiring for the evening without a care for the state of the room. She supposed she would have done much the same if she were staying in a place she didn't call home, involuntarily, where people were around to pick up the mess left behind. She'd placed the last board game in its slot on a shelf when Violet rushed in, tears drying in tracks down her cheeks.

"Violet! What are you still doing here? You should have gone home hours ago!"

"I know, Willy. I just couldn't leave. Natalie was so despondent all day. I was too afraid to leave her alone. And now she's ranting. She started screaming at me that she wanted to see you."

Wilhelmina followed Violet up to the third floor at a run, the panic emanating from the young girl spurring the head nurse faster than she'd ever moved through Tranquil Heights. The door to Natalie's room was open, and she was pacing from one side of the room to the other, still dressed in a hospital gown, muttering under her breath in clipped words. She came to a dead stop as she saw Wilhelmina cross the threshold.

"Natalie, dear, you should really be resting." Wilhelmina crossed to Natalie, placing an arm around her shoulders, ready to usher her back to bed.

Natalie shook Wilhelmina's arms off, stepping just out of reach, shaking her head back and forth in an exaggerated fashion. "No, I've been resting all day. Lying in bed and thinking about this morning."

"Of course. I wouldn't expect you not to think about it." Wilhelmina held her hands out in front of her, ready to physically intervene if Natalie collapsed. Natalie began pacing again, though she never took her eyes off Wilhelmina. She reminded the nurse of the tigers in cages on the traveling circus trains, pacing restlessly, waiting for the moment they could pounce.

"How long did you know, Wilhelmina?"

"Natalie, let's just take a moment to calm down and we can sit and have this conversation."

"HOW LONG, WILHELMINA!?" Natalie's voice cracked with the force of her scream.

The air in the room took on that thick quality that Wilhelmina had convinced herself she'd imagined. A movement at the door caught her attention, and Wilhelmina turned to see Violet trying to sneak away.

"No, Violet, stay. You'll learn a valuable lesson about trust," Natalie said. Violet hesitated, looking to Wilhelmina to tell her what to do. "Get in the room and close the door, Violet." Natalie's voice dropped to a low, commanding purr.

Violet tripped into the room and the door slammed behind her, though Wilhelmina didn't see Violet's hands on it. She rushed to Wilhelmina and threw herself into the older woman's arms, seeking comfort. Both of them focused on Natalie, faces drained, eyes wide.

"I'm waiting, Wilhelmina."

"Dr. Covington got a letter with the envelope that had your train ticket."

"And when did Dr. Covington tell you?"

"The day after you got the ticket," Wilhelmina answered in a whisper after a long pause.

"And why didn't you tell me?" Natalie's voice was a forced calm, but the pressure in the room grew, and Wilhelmina had the wild thought that this was the calm before the storm.

"Dr. Covington was concerned about the impact the news would have on you in such a late stage of your pregnancy. He was worried for both you and the baby."

"And you agreed?"

"I did. I know how much you wanted that baby, Natalie. I knew it would destroy you to find out."

"So, you decided for me. Just like the senator."

"No! No, no, no," Wilhelmina's voice cracked, and tears spilled onto her cheeks. "I did it because I care about you. If I had told you, and the shock hurt you, I'd never forgive myself. And if the shock had hurt the baby, neither of us would have ever forgiven me."

"But I could have run, Wilhelmina. I could have gotten out of here, gone far away where the Cumberlands couldn't find me. I could be somewhere else holding my baby right now."

"It was too risky, Natalie."

"No, Wilhelmina. It wasn't too risky. You are just a coward." Natalie's voice was venomous and her anger bit along Wilhelmina's skin like a colony of fire ants. "All you had to do was be a good friend and tell me the truth. I could have my baby, and I could be happy. But you lied to me, for weeks. And now I am alone."

Wilhelmina openly wept. She couldn't argue, she had second guessed her decision every minute of every day of the last few weeks of Natalie's pregnancy. Now, in this room, surrounded by Natalie's anger and grief, she even agreed that she was responsible for Natalie's loss. She had ultimately chosen not to tell Natalie because that was Dr. Covington's order. Wilhelmina realized in that moment that she had valued the security of this job more than she had valued the bond she'd formed with Natalie.

"I am so sorry, Natalie. So, so, sorry. But you aren't alone. Not if you don't want to be."

"What, are you going to tell me I have you? The woman who betrayed me?" Natalie's voice was full of derision and she laughed, a bitter, hollow sound. "No, Wilhelmina, you don't get absolution that easily."

"I know. I know what I've done is beyond forgiveness. But I can still help you, I can still be your friend."

"No, Wilhelmina, you can't. Everything I wanted from life, everything I am, you have taken from me. You have killed me, Wilhelmina Darrington."

A hot wind tore Wilhelmina's hair from her bun and filled the room with the smell of a summer storm. The thick, heady smell of rain sat on the back of Wilhelmina's throat, choking her. The sound of the wind filled her ears, and she could feel herself shouting into that wind, but it carried her voice away into nothingness. Violet's hair whipped around her face, her eyes were wide, and her hands mottled with red splotches where they gripped Wilhelmina's arm tightly.

Wilhelmina felt something well up insider her—a resolve to stop the madness, a need to stop the heat from engulfing her. She thought of winter, of snow and frozen ponds. The wind suddenly stopped, and the temperature plummeted the way it does at night as the sun sets. The whooshing of Wilhelmina's own heartbeat replaced the howling of the wind, and a high mewling sound coming from Violet. The window on the left side of the room opened with a violent rattle that should have dislodged the panes. Wilhelmina watched Natalie step towards the window. It was like everything slowed down, like the world was moving through molasses. Wilhelmina threw her hand out, though she knew there was no chance she could get to Natalie in time. Natalie turned just as she made it to the window and made direct eye contact with Wilhelmina.

"Life has a way of balancing itself, Wilhelmina."

"NO!" Wilhelmina shouted and lurched forward.

Time seemed to have gone back to normal and Wilhelmina's hand grasped the air where just seconds before had been Natalie. Violet rushed up next to Wilhelmina, and they both looked out the window. Violet let out a strangled cry and buried her head in Wilhelmina's chest. Wilhelmina hugged Violet tight to her, hands rubbing in soothing circles, though her eyes stayed on the body of Natalie Arthur in the grass below.

She watched as orderlies rushed to her, medical bags in hand. But it was too late. She knew that Natalie Arthur was dead because she could see a shining, transparent version of the woman staring up at her, just steps away from the body.

TWENTY-SIX

KATIE LOOKED UP FROM THE PAGES of the journal to find Violet Camden crying. Katie wiped the tears away from her own cheeks and placed the pages face down in her lap. She couldn't bear to look at them.

"Poor Wilhelmina," Jason said, voice gruff.

"Poor Natalie," Katie replied.

"Poor Natalie?" he questioned. "I'm sorry, but doesn't it sound like she's the one who cursed your family, Katie."

"It sounds that way, yes." Katie sighed. "But she was distraught, Jason. She was literally hours postpartum, after delivering a baby she loved and wanted. And that baby was taken from her. After Wilhelmina let her believe she was going to get to keep that baby."

"So, you agree with Wilhelmina? She was to blame and your family deserves what it got?"

"No, I don't agree with Wilhelmina. But I'm not as close to the situation. I didn't watch that poor woman throw herself out a window."

"For what it's worth, I didn't agree with Wilhelmina either. And I did watch Natalie throw herself out a window," Violet said, tucking a tissue back into the sleeve of her sweater.

"Why didn't you come forward and find my family?"

"Because I promised Wilhelmina to always keep the secret. And who would have believed me? Curses, and magic, whatever Natalie had? It all seems like a fantastic story, but not real. But I'm at the end of my life, and you came seeking me. Though, if the curse really has taken hold of your family as Wilhelmina feared, I'm not really sure what telling the secret does to help you."

"I do," Katie said, voice hard. "Thank you, Violet, for giving me this." She stood and looked at Jason and Darla. "We have a ghost to contact." She strode from the room, head held high and body filled with a warmth that told her she was on the right track.

Annie followed them out on the porch, tear tracks drying on her cheeks. "I want you to know that my great-grandma became a nurse. She fought her entire career for equality for women in healthcare. I never knew why she was so adamant about it. I thought she was just ahead of her time in terms of feminism. Now I know, it's because of what happened to that woman in the journal entry. Because she never should have had her baby taken away." She shook her head and stared at her toes for a long moment. "But your family isn't to blame. My great-grandma isn't to blame. She and Wilhelmina were as much victims of the system as Natalie was. I hope you're able to fix this for your family."

. . .

Herbs burned in room 302 at Tranquil Heights. The smoke made lazy curls in the air above the bowls in which they burned. A white candle sat in a pile of salt upon a pretty floral plate, waiting to be lit.

A photo of an old woman surrounded by younger people who looked like her and small children, all smiling happily, sat between the herbs and candle. A name had been listed on the back of the letter Wilhelmina had sent to Violet in a different handwriting. Katie and Darla had searched for the name Laura Peterson among the records of the museum and found that it was a baby who had been born at Tranquil Heights in 1935 and put up for adoption. Further searching had them convinced that the woman in the photo was Natalie Arthur's baby.

After all, how many baby girls could have been born at Tranquil Heights on May 14, 1935?

Katie, Jason and Darla stood over the small altar, breathing in the scent of the herbs and trying to calm their nerves. They stared out the window and watched the sun sink lower below the trees. Katie thought about the sound of that window latch sliding open in the dead of night, the way it had crashed open the night she'd tried to contact Liz. She felt Jason shudder next to him and knew he was thinking of the same thing.

They watched as the last glimmer of red blinked out and darkness claimed the grounds outside the window. Katie stepped forward and lit the white candle. She stepped back in line with Jason and Darla and grabbed their hands.

"Natalie Arthur, we'd like to speak to you, if you'd be willing."

At first, nothing happened. Katie opened her mouth to ask again when the room temperature dropped. She let out a shaky breath, watching the plumes of fog swirl in front of her face from the hot air she released. She felt Jason and Darla shudder next to her. They cast their eyes around the room, searching for The White Lady but seeing nothing.

"Natalie, can you show yourself, please?"

Katie hadn't thought it was possible, but the room got even colder. She was convinced that if they stood there in the cold much longer, they'd suffer from hypothermia and perish, three more ghosts for Tranquil Heights. A hot gust of air rushed past Katie's head, sending her hair into her face and leaving a tingling pain much like when you wash your icy hands in a hot stream of water after playing in the snow. Next came a gust of cold air, then hot, then cold, until the three of them stood in a gale of alternating hot and cold air. The blasts were so sharp they felt as though they were leaving cuts along Katie's skin. Darla and Jason cried out in pain on either side of her, though physically they all looked whole and healthy.

"What's happening?" Darla screamed over the sound of the wind.

"I don't know. It wasn't like this last time," Katie answered. "Natalie, please! I just want to talk to you. I need you to know what happened to you wasn't Wilhelmina's fault, or yours. It was the world's fault!"

The wind slowed, and the temperature slowly normalized, though it remained cold enough to raise goosebumps. The trio let out shaky breaths in tandem, relieved that at least they weren't being hurt by the wind anymore. Katie could feel the pulse of both Darla and Jason through their hands like trapped things trying to escape.

The White Lady appeared before them just inside the window. Jason's pulse sped, pounding out a frantic beat against Katie's hand. Natalie watched them, expression hidden by the glow that emanated from her.

"Wilhelmina had a child to care for. She needed the job. It seems like a selfish choice, to not tell you about the baby being taken. Even I can admit to thinking it seems selfish. But finding a job was so hard in the 1930s. You should know that. And to find one as a woman?" Katie let out a bitter laugh. "Wilhelmina made a choice that protected her family. That protected her baby. And when you put it that way, that's actually pretty selfless."

The White Lady—Natalie—turned her head to look at something in the room's corner. Katie's eyes followed, but she saw nothing. Katie shook it off, assuming that Natalie was reliving some memory and watching it unfold before her eyes. She broke away from Jason and Darla to pick up the photo. Natalie turned back to her, and Katie got the sense that she was wary. Katie moved slowly, an animal attempting not to spook the predator, and showed Natalie the photo.

"This woman in the center of this photo is Laura Peterson. She's your daughter. She's lived a really incredible life. She became a lawyer, and she had three children. She has sixteen grandchildren and four great-grandchildren. She's happy. She's had a happy life. A full life."

The temperature dropped again, and Katie

frantically dug her phone from her pocket, pulling up the photo of her and Liz once again. She held the phone up toward Natalie.

"This is my sister Liz. She died a month ago on our twenty-fifth birthday. She looked just like Wilhelmina, and she was my universe. Part of me is lost and empty without her. And she'll never get to have kids, or grandkids, or great-grandkids. She won't get to live a full life. Just like my Aunt Anita, and my grandmother's sister Mary, and their mother, Wilhelmina's daughter, Eleanor. Your baby was torn away from you, your family torn apart before it could even start. My family's been torn apart, too, by generations of grief, and anger, and guilt. Wilhelmina wasn't responsible for tearing apart your family, and I don't really think you're responsible for tearing apart mine."

Katie had a strange sensation, like being split in half. One half of her body was cold, the other warm, approaching hot. She closed her eyes, overwhelmed by the sensation, trying to make sense of what she was feeling. When she opened her eyes again, Natalie was standing closer, and some of the bright glow around her had died down. Her eyes were sad, and Katie choked out a sob.

"I'm going to have a baby. And I think it's going to be a girl. I want her to live a full life. I want her to share her power with the world, like I know you could have if you'd had better circumstances." Katie held her hands protectively over her stomach and watched as tears spilled down Natalie Arthur's cheeks. She had a moment to be surprised that ghosts could cry before the room plunged into darkness, the only light the flickering of the small white candle and the glow of Natalie. The room became so cold that it drove Katie to her knees, and a terrible shrieking noise started that made her clap her hands over her ears. She turned enough to see that both Jason and Darla were also on their knees and clutching their heads.

She looked up to see Natalie's mouth open, like it had been the first night Katie had seen her on the grounds below the window. The wind picked up as it had the night she'd contacted Liz, hot and fast, building a funnel around them.

"Natalie, please!" Katie screamed, throat burning with the effort to be loud enough to be heard over the howling wind. "Don't you see? You and Wilhelmina were both victims of a society that didn't care about its women, who treated them as crazy when they'd done nothing wrong. That hid them away when they were too smart, too powerful, when they could topple the men at the top of the food chain. Please, please, letting more powerful women die before they've lived their full potential won't undo what happened to you."

Katie was sobbing, and it took her a moment to understand that the screaming had stopped. The wind slowed, and the room took on a pleasant warmth, like a day on the beach in the sun. Katie watched Natalie, who was once again staring off at a corner of the room, seeing things no one else could.

"We were so blind," she said, still not looking at Katie. "It's time." She turned the full force of her gaze to Katie and stepped forward, right hand outreached. Katie got to her feet and took a step forward, but a hand caught hold of her left wrist. She turned to look at Jason, whose panic-stricken eyes pleaded with her not to go to the ghost.

"It's okay, Jason." She smiled at him and nodded.

"Are you sure?"

"I've never been more sure of anything."

Jason's hand dropped away. A look on his face said plainly that he was not at all sure it was the right decision, but he let her go.

Katie turned back to Natalie, smile still upon her face, and she was surprised to find that Natalie was smiling back. They each took one more step forward, and Natalie's soft white light enveloped Katie. Natalie's hand settled gently against the left side of Katie's face, and Katie had to fight to not close her eyes against the brightness. Her eyes met Natalie's, and she felt as though she were both weightless and falling, but she felt no fear.

"Change the world for me, Katie Edgecomb," Natalie whispered, and then all was black.

TWENTY-SEVEN

KATIE AND JASON'S COUNTRY COTTAGE was filled with people. They'd chosen to move out of the city after their experience at Tranquil Heights. Katie wanted a yard in which their daughter could play with a dog, and Jason had agreed that the fresh air and trees were more appealing to him than the concrete and tall buildings of the city.

A pink banner above the fireplace read "Welcome Home, Elizabeth Natalie Edgecomb." Katie smiled as she watched her little bundle of pink blankets passed around the room. It seemed like everyone they'd ever known was packed into the small house, but Katie was okay with that. As far as Katie was concerned, Elizabeth was the greatest thing that had ever happened in the history of humankind and everyone else should have the chance to know that, too.

Darla sat across from her at the kitchen table, telling Jason about her capstone work regarding haunted buildings across America. Jason still couldn't help but scoff at the idea of ghosts and hauntings being a proper thing to research for academic purposes, even after his own encounter with The White Lady. Darla shrugged off his continued skepticism and continued to visit every Friday night. Katie supposed you couldn't investigate a curse and contact a ghost together without becoming the best of friends. No matter the reason for the friendship, she was glad to have a friend who understood her.

A hand crossed in front of Katie's vision and reached for the ladle in the punchbowl, making Katie jump. She swiveled her head to look at her mother, who immediately dropped the ladle.

"Oh Katie, I'm so sorry. I keep forgetting that I can't come at you from the left side anymore."

"It's okay, Mom."

"I still don't understand. How did a ghost simply touching you make you lose your sight?"

"I'm not one hundred percent sure I understand it myself, Mom."

"But if she saw the error of her ways and wanted to lift the curse, why would she turn around and injure you?"

"I don't think she did it, Mom."

"Of course she did it, Katie. She touched you, and you woke up with no sight in your left eye."

"You weren't there. You didn't see it or feel it. You didn't form that connection with Natalie. She didn't want to hurt me. I don't think she wanted to hurt anyone."

"Katie, she cursed this family for four generations. How can you say she didn't want to hurt this family?"

"I don't think she realized exactly what she'd done, Mom. She was distraught, her world had been torn from her. In that moment, everything focused down into grief. Are you really telling me if you had someone in front of you that you could rationally blame for your child being taken, that you wouldn't wish them ill?"

"Well, I certainly wouldn't wish them the pain of losing a child," Angela said with a sniff.

"Mom, when we came home and explained how the curse came to be, and how we contacted Natalie and how it was broken, you literally said to me 'I hope that bitch burns in hell.' I don't think you can pretend to take the high road here."

"But it's not over, Katie. You can't see out of one eye. She couldn't lift the curse without taking a parting shot. I kind of think we are on the high road."

"You just don't get it. Natalie didn't intentionally do this to me. It just happened. It's like... because I could see so much of the truth. To see what happened in 1935, how Wilhelmina and Natalie were victims, together. I don't know… I've seen too much. More than anyone was meant to, and certainly more than Natalie and Wilhelmina could. Natalie said they'd been blind, and I helped her overcome that blindness. I think life had to balance out and take a little bit of sight from me because of it."

Angela's chest puffed and she opened her mouth to argue further, but Jason held up his hand to stop her. "It's best we just let the dead rest, Angela."

EPILOGUE

DARLA NEWKIRK STOOD OVER THE GRAVE of Natalie Arthur, taking in the bouquet of pink roses and the crocheted afghan of many colors that Katie Edgecomb had left as a tribute to the long deceased. A striking woman with white blonde hair and blue eyes so clear and light they looked like ice stood next to her, hands clasped in front of her.

"I thought when they were free, I'd be free," she said.

"I thought so, too," replied Darla.

"And yet?"

"And yet."

ACKNOWLEDGEMENTS

Thank you to Megan Harris, who helped me catch all the little mistakes. Thanks to Jo McCall for being an amazing cheerleader and compatriot. Thank you to my team of beta readers who helped me fill in holes and showed me where they were the most impacted by my words. Thanks Kori and Maxine for dealing with my obsession over this book over several months.

And thank you to you, who bought this book.

ABOUT THE AUTHOR

Megan is a writer, horror buff, and dog person. She is currently writing books and helping authors navigate self publishing. She lives in the beautiful Pacific Northwest with her husband and two dogs, and can be found spending her weekends at the beach, exploring everything Washington has to offer, or settling in with a good horror movie.

Megan Speece Writes

@meganspeecewrites

@meganspeecewrites

@mbspeece

Sign up for the newsletter and
never miss an important update:

www.meganspeecewrites.com

www.ingramcontent.com/pod-product-compliance
Lightning Source LLC
Chambersburg PA
CBHW022024120726
47898CB00007BA/2459